FOX & RABBIT

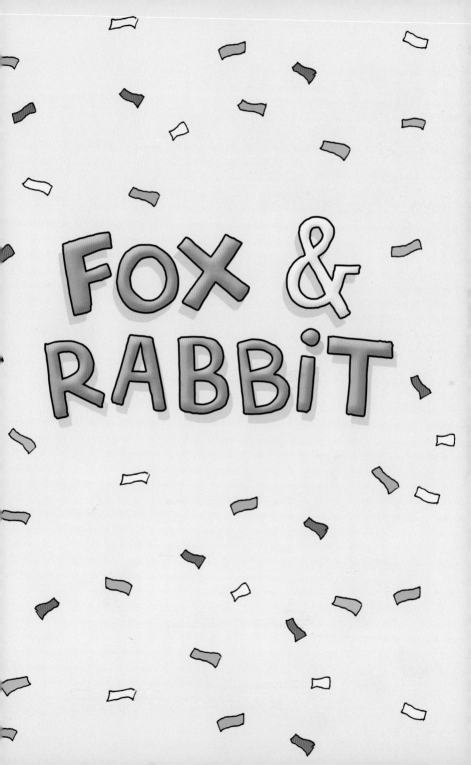

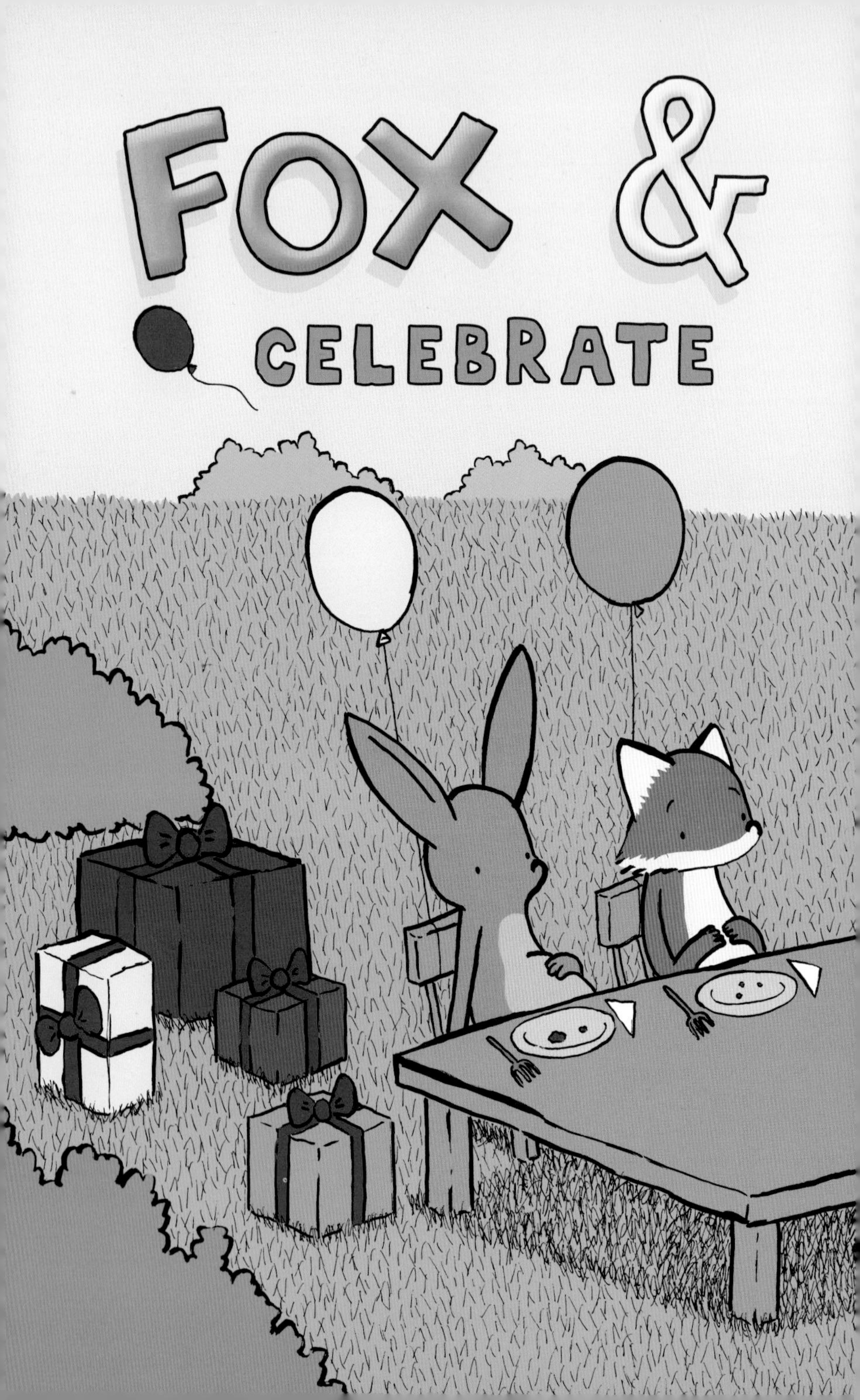
FOX &
CELEBRATE

RABBIT

by Beth Ferry

illustrated by Gergely Dudás

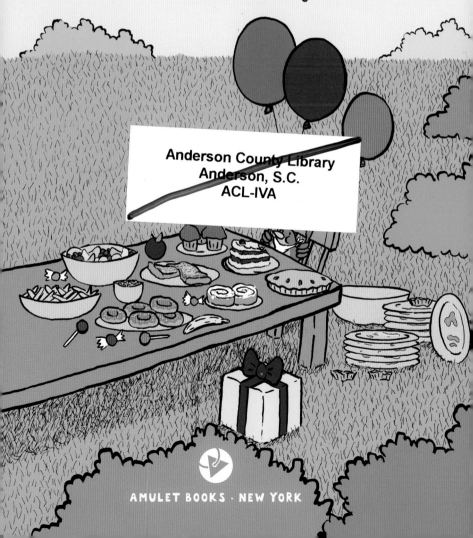

AMULET BOOKS · NEW YORK

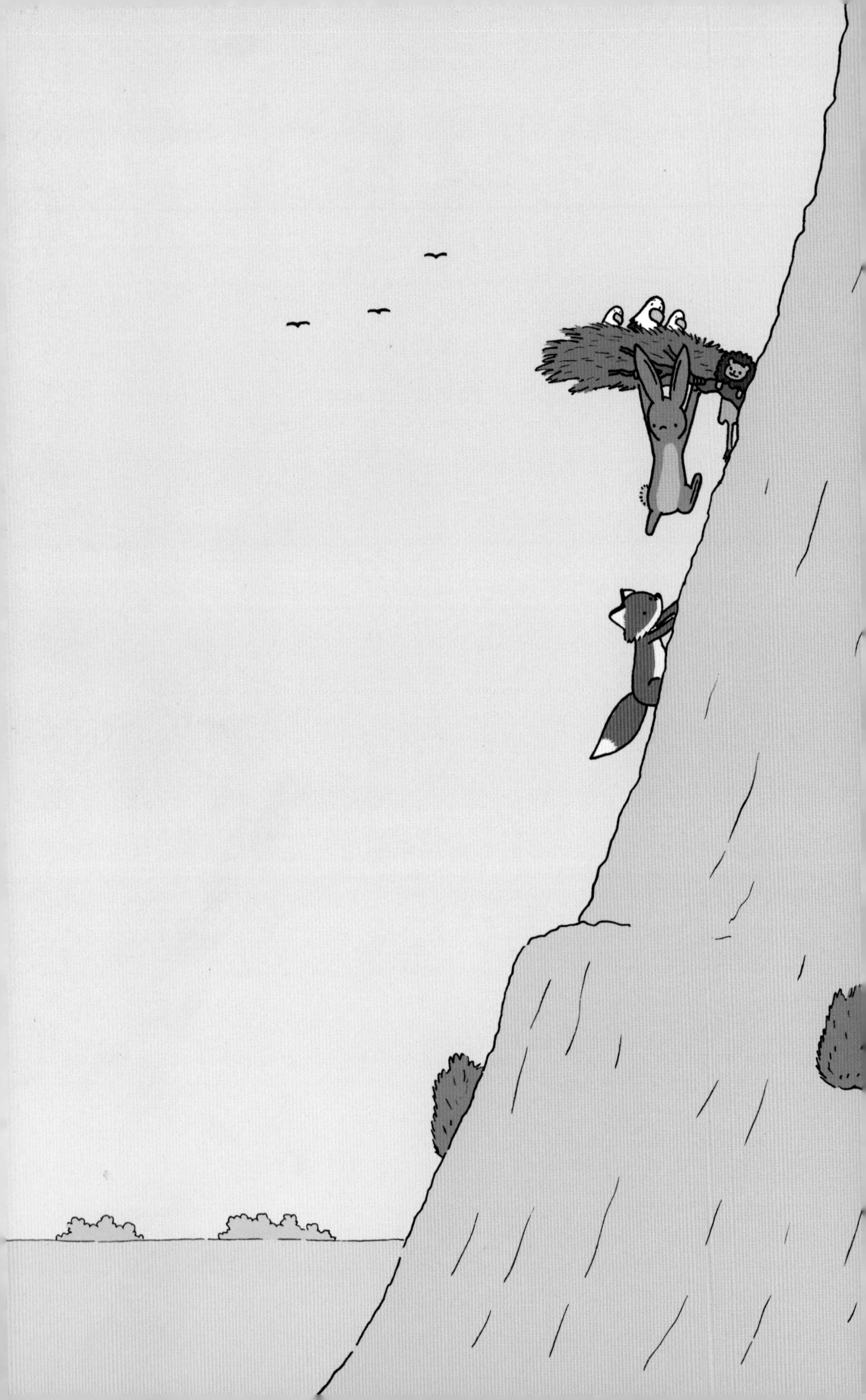

CONTENTS

STORY ONE

FIX, FUSS & FLIES

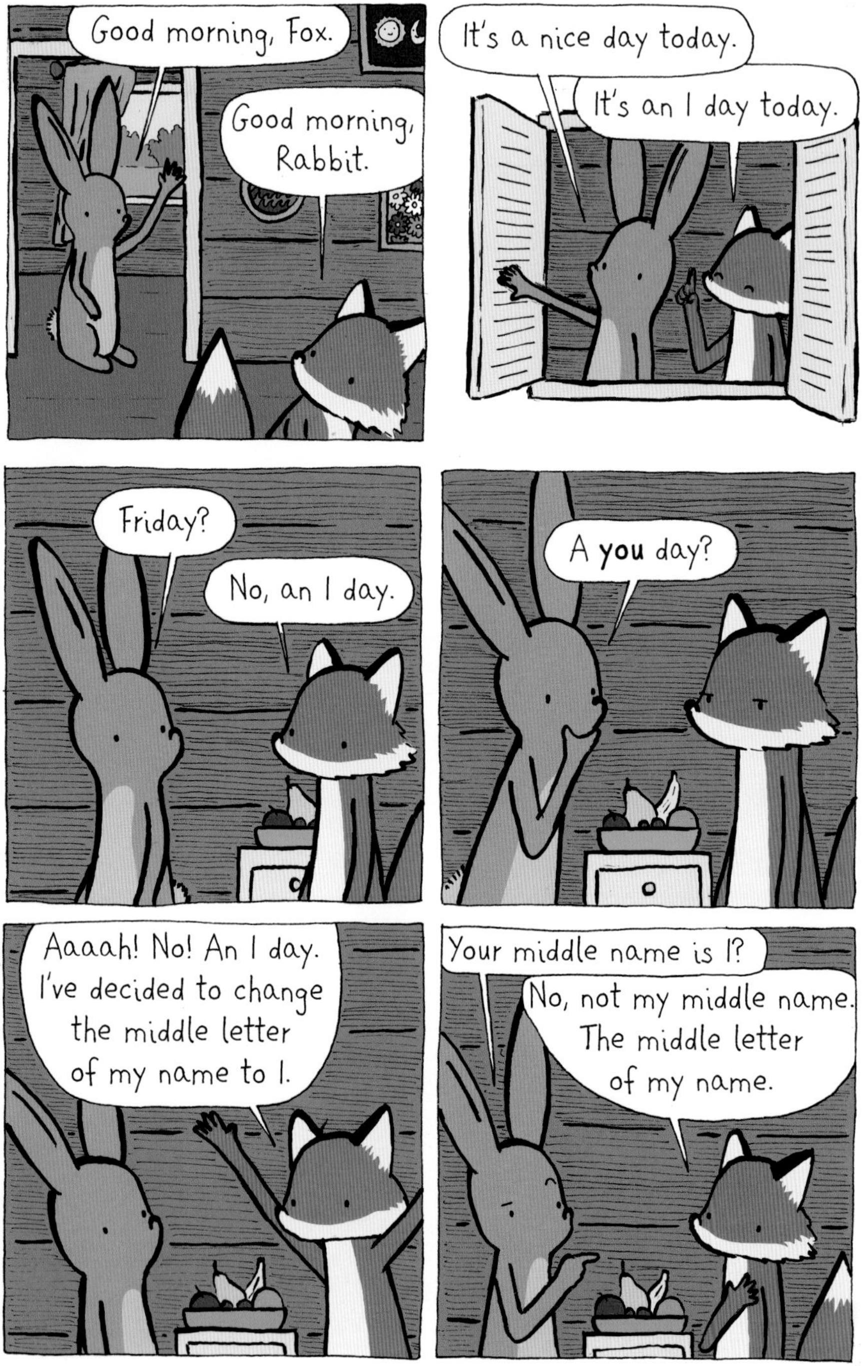
Good morning, Fox.
Good morning, Rabbit.
It's a nice day today.
It's an I day today.
Friday?
No, an I day.
A **you** day?
Aaaah! No! An I day. I've decided to change the middle letter of my name to I.
Your middle name is I?
No, not my middle name. The middle letter of my name.

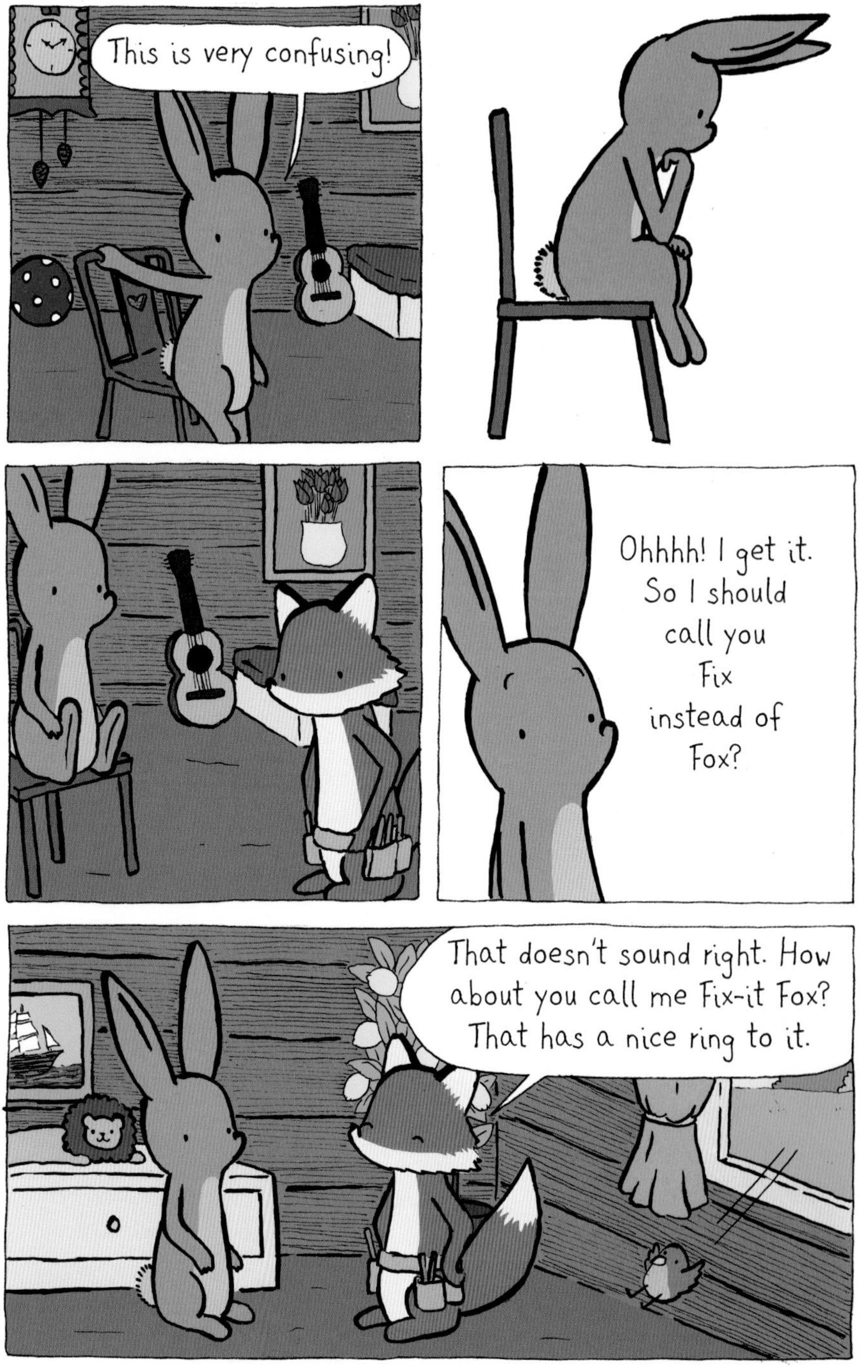
This is very confusing!
Ohhhh! I get it. So I should call you Fix instead of Fox?
That doesn't sound right. How about you call me Fix-it Fox? That has a nice ring to it.

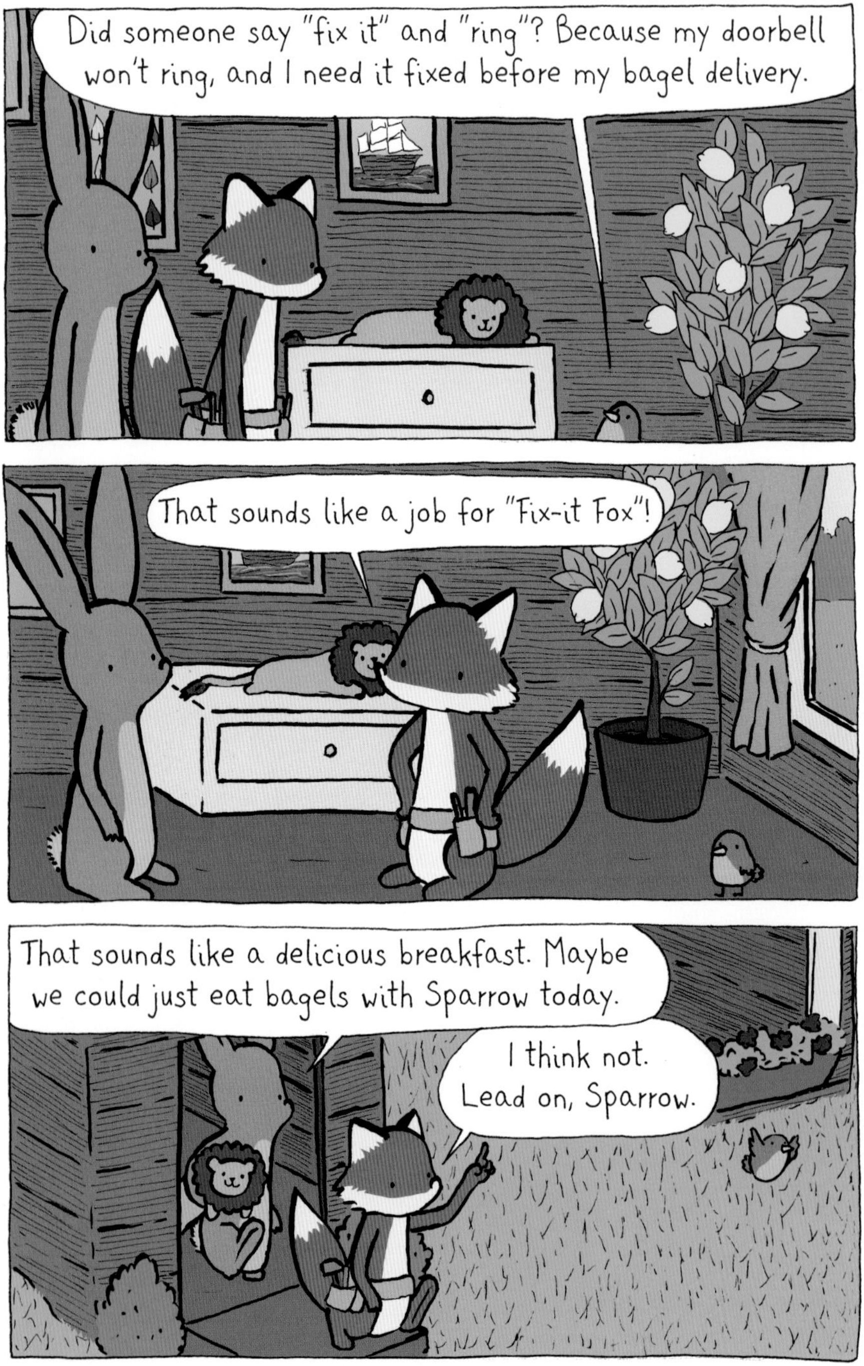
Did someone say "fix it" and "ring"? Because my doorbell won't ring, and I need it fixed before my bagel delivery.
That sounds like a job for "Fix-it Fox"!
That sounds like a delicious breakfast. Maybe we could just eat bagels with Sparrow today.
I think not. Lead on, Sparrow.

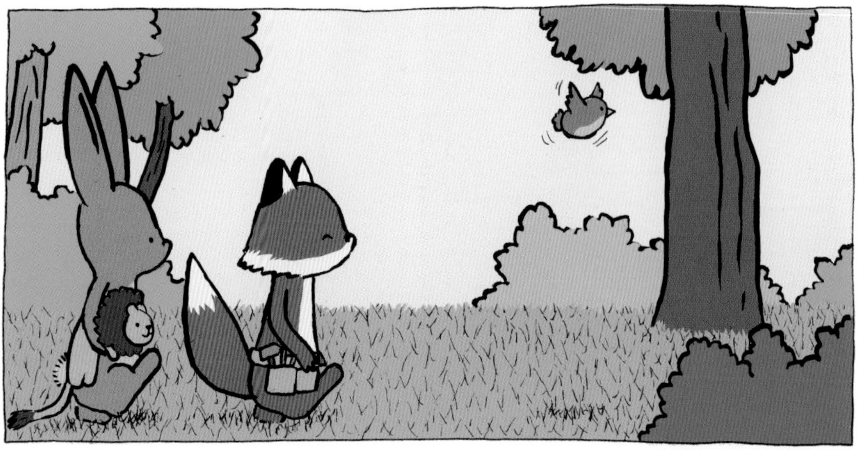

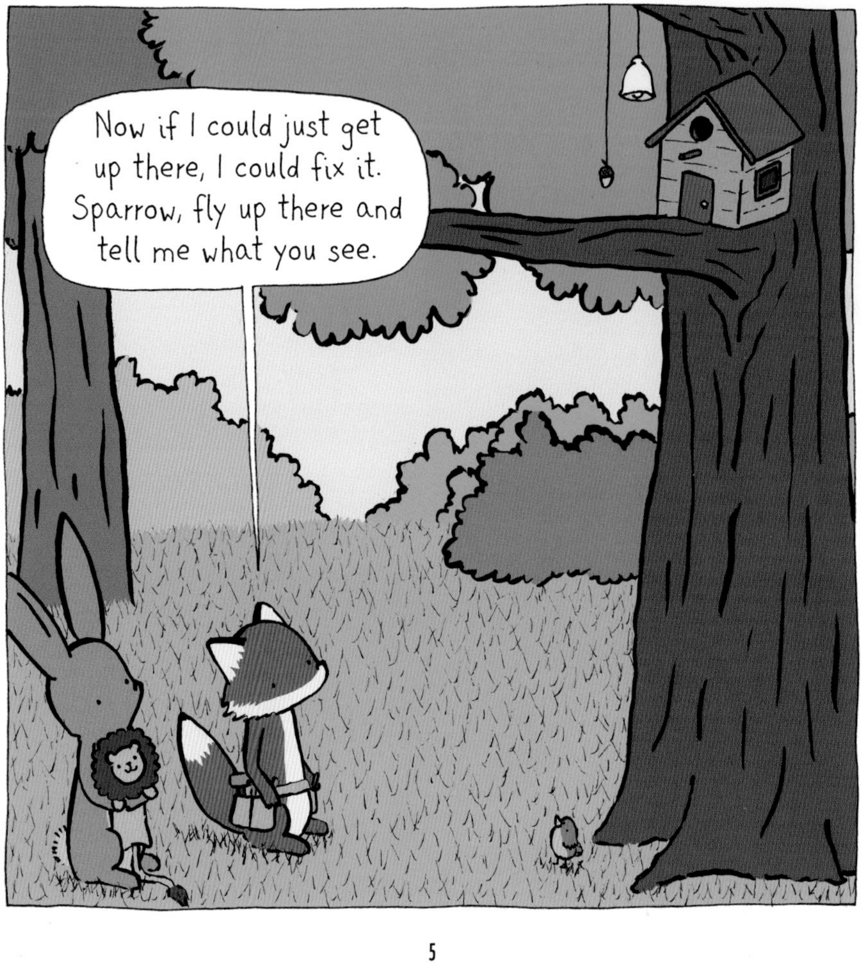
Now if I could just get up there, I could fix it. Sparrow, fly up there and tell me what you see.

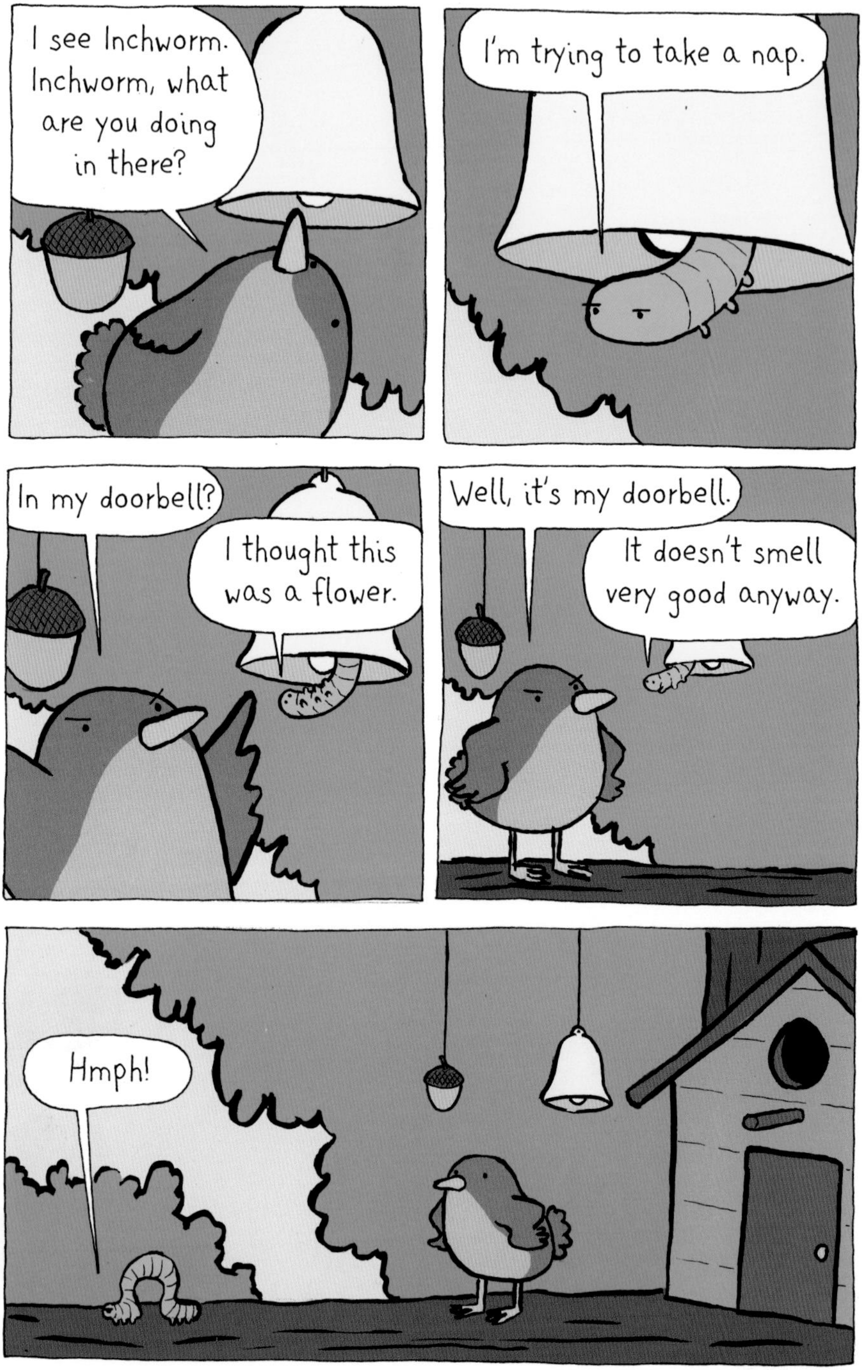
I see Inchworm. Inchworm, what are you doing in there?
I'm trying to take a nap.
In my doorbell?
I thought this was a flower.
Well, it's my doorbell.
It doesn't smell very good anyway.
Hmph!

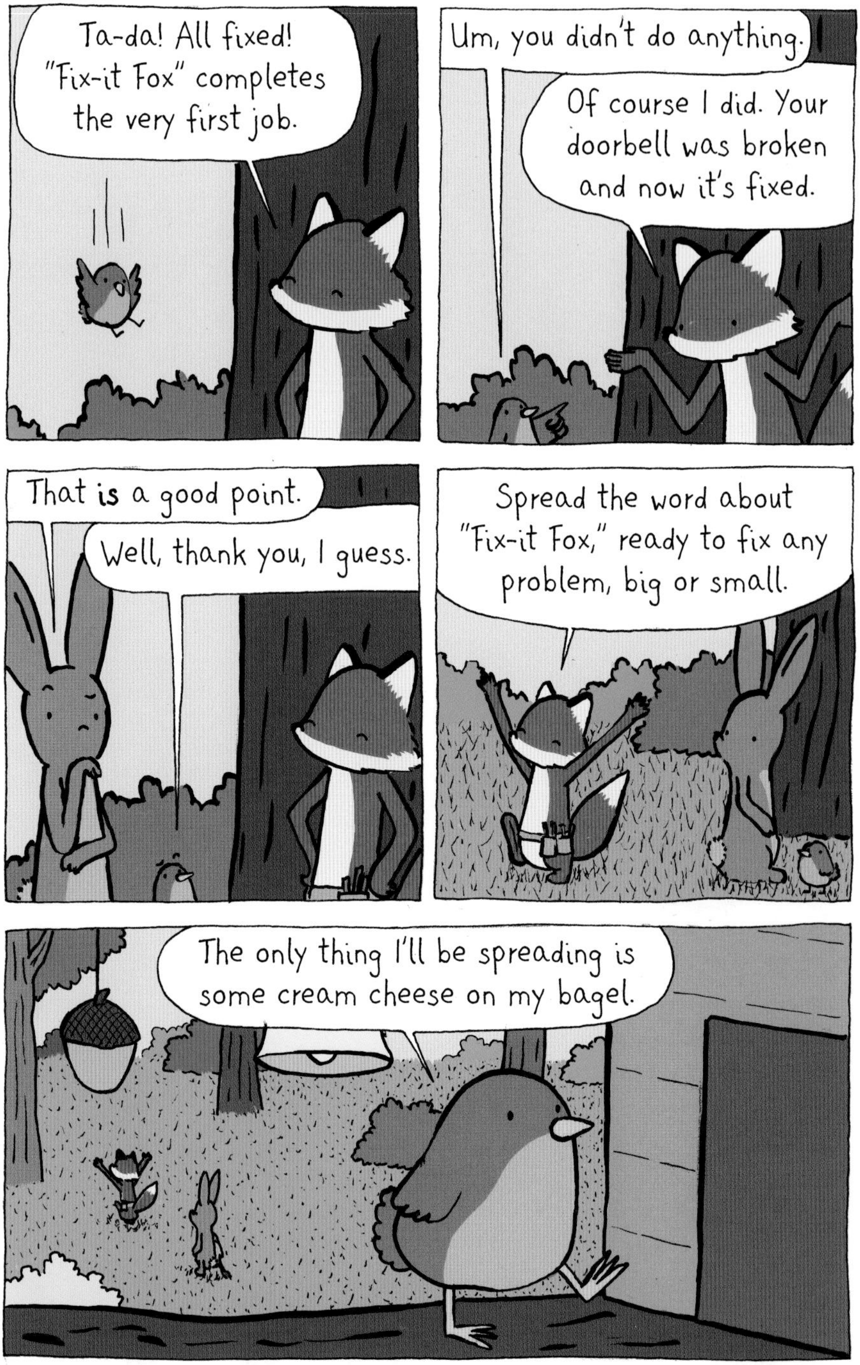
Ta-da! All fixed! "Fix-it Fox" completes the very first job.
Um, you didn't do anything.
Of course I did. Your doorbell was broken and now it's fixed.
That **is** a good point.
Well, thank you, I guess.
Spread the word about "Fix-it Fox," ready to fix any problem, big or small.
The only thing I'll be spreading is some cream cheese on my bagel.

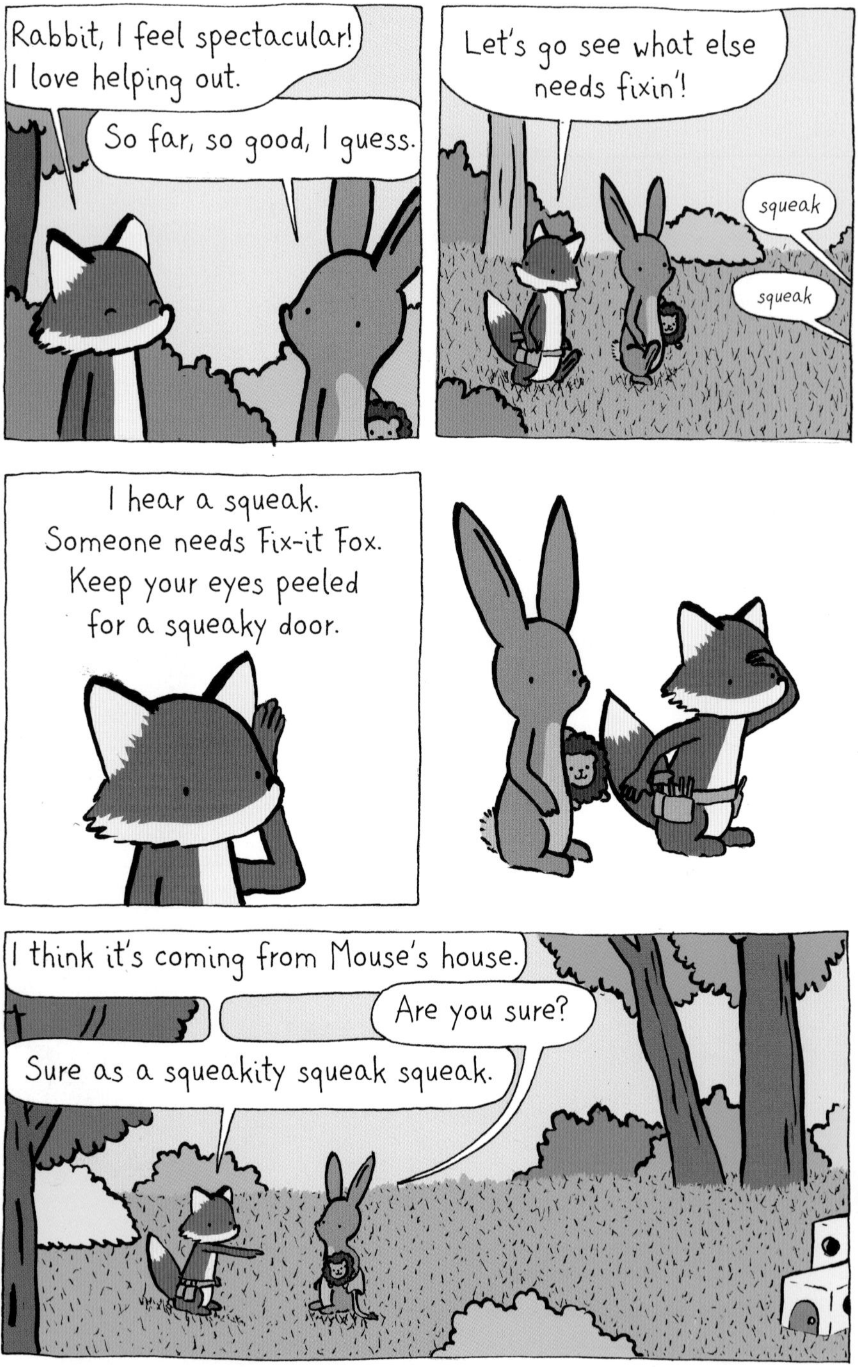
Rabbit, I feel spectacular! I love helping out.
So far, so good, I guess.
Let's go see what else needs fixin'!
squeak
squeak
I hear a squeak. Someone needs Fix-it Fox. Keep your eyes peeled for a squeaky door.
I think it's coming from Mouse's house.
Are you sure?
Sure as a squeakity squeak squeak.

Aha! That little door probably hasn't been oiled in years. One little squirt should do it.

squeak

Hmmm, maybe a little more.

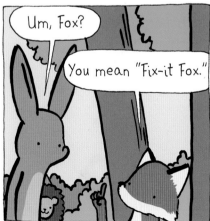
Um, Fox?

You mean "Fix-it Fox."

Um, Fix-it Fox?

Let me just try one more thing.

CRACK!

That's better. I don't hear any more squeaking.

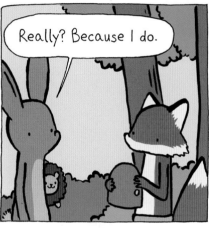

Really? Because I do.

squeak

squeak

Um, Fox, I don't think the squeaks were coming from the door. I think they were coming from the mice.

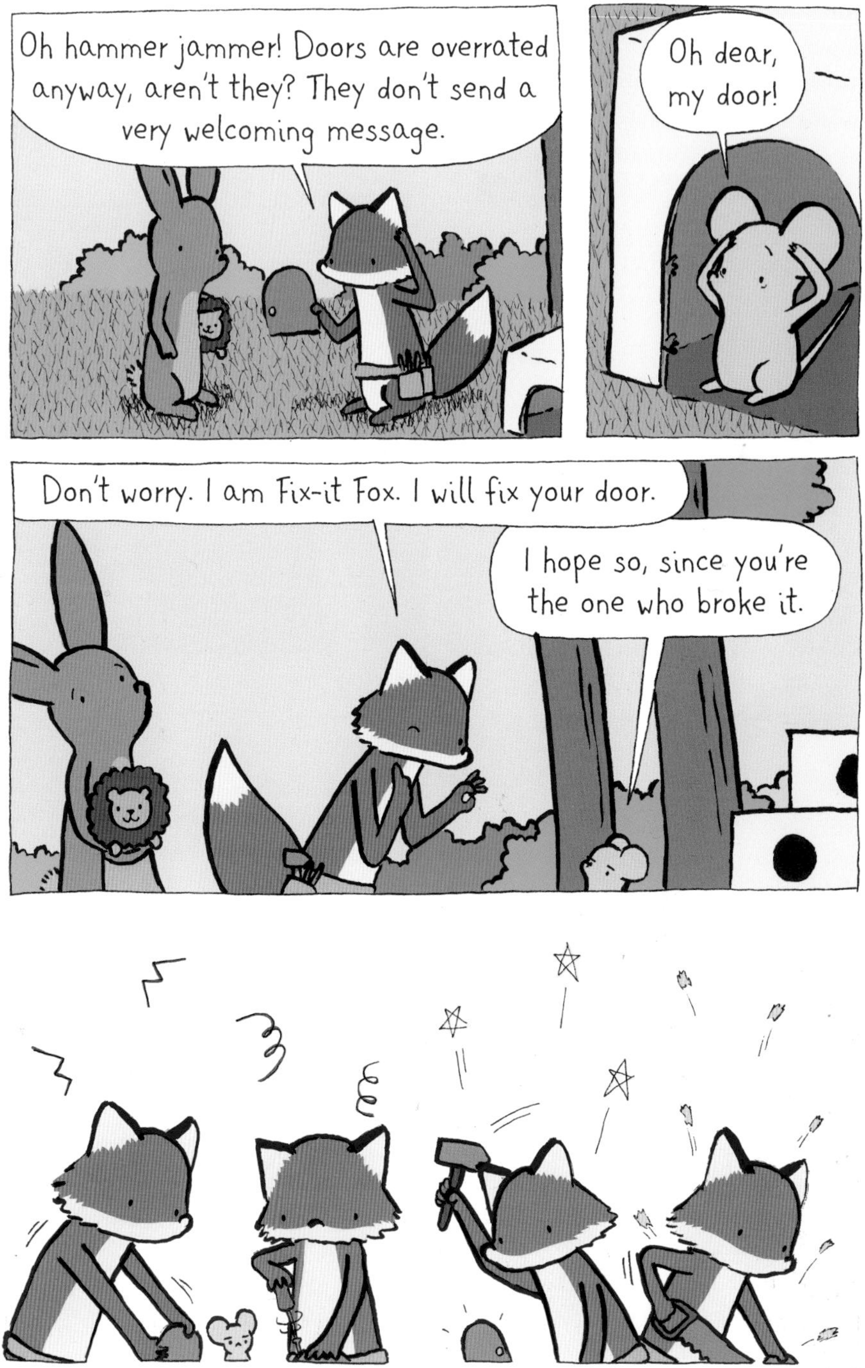
Oh hammer jammer! Doors are overrated anyway, aren't they? They don't send a very welcoming message.
Oh dear, my door!
Don't worry. I am Fix-it Fox. I will fix your door.
I hope so, since you're the one who broke it.

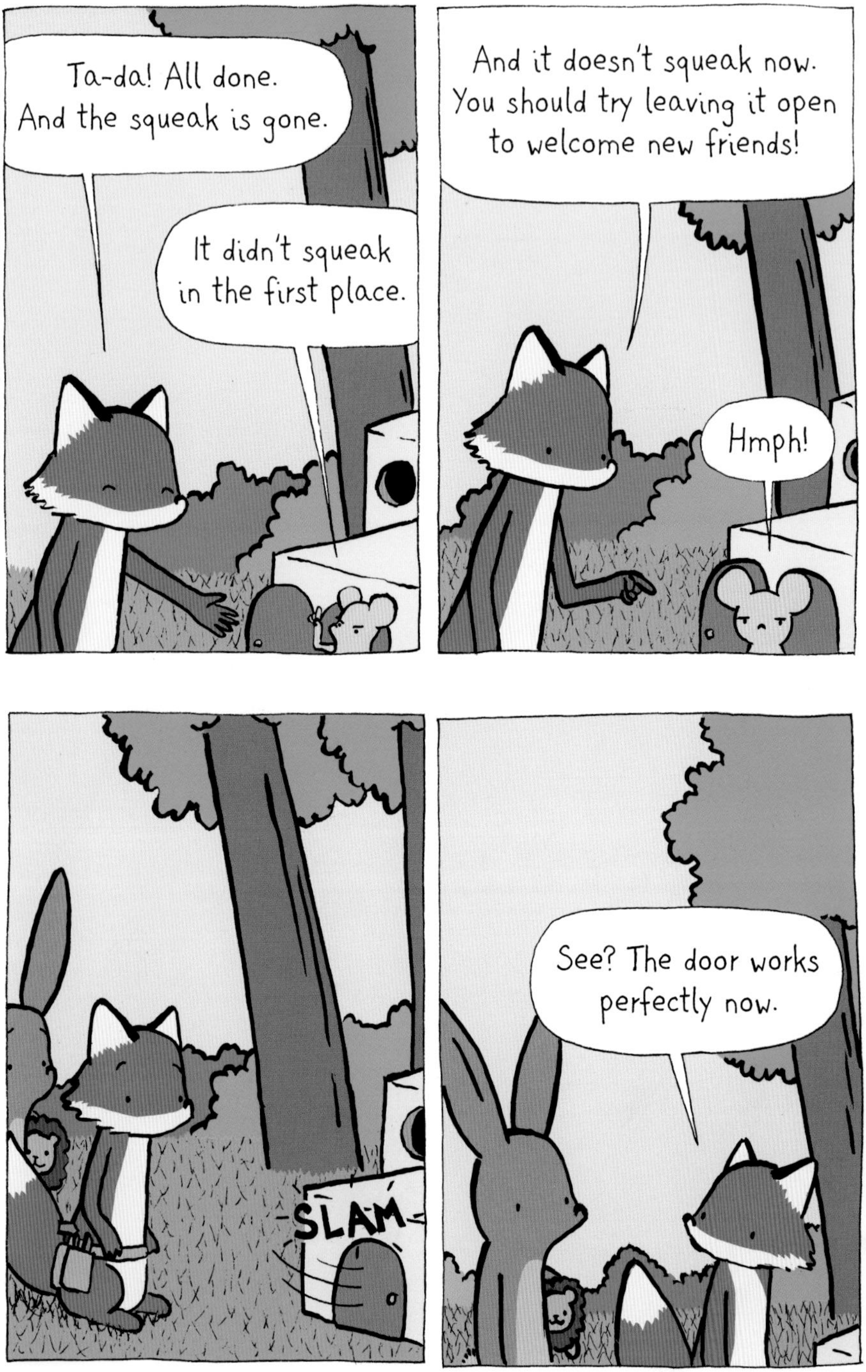
Ta-da! All done.
And the squeak is gone.
It didn't squeak
in the first place.
And it doesn't squeak now.
You should try leaving it open
to welcome new friends!
Hmph!
SLAM
See? The door works
perfectly now.

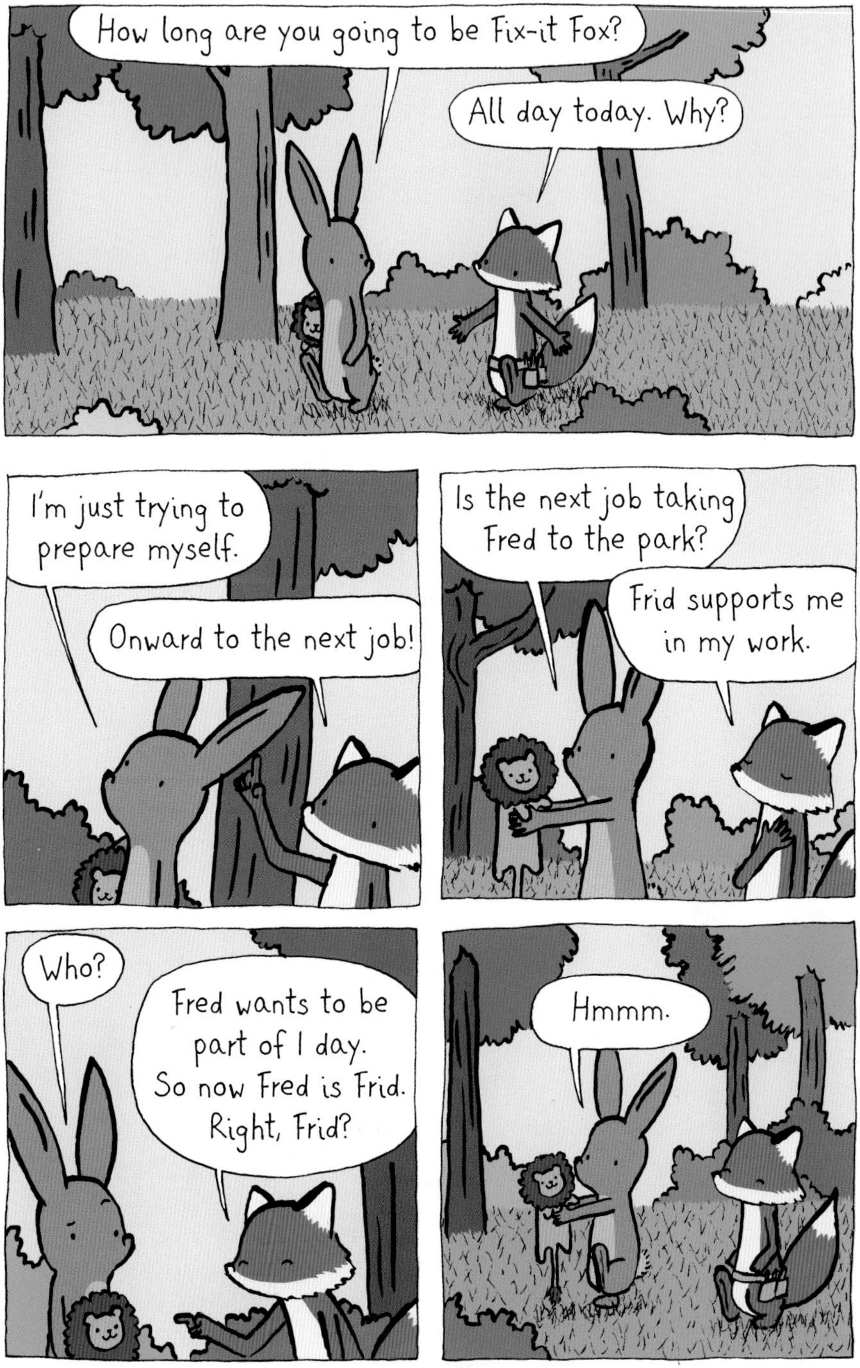
How long are you going to be Fix-it Fox?
All day today. Why?
I'm just trying to prepare myself.
Onward to the next job!
Is the next job taking Fred to the park?
Frid supports me in my work.
Who?
Fred wants to be part of 1 day. So now Fred is Frid. Right, Frid?
Hmmm.

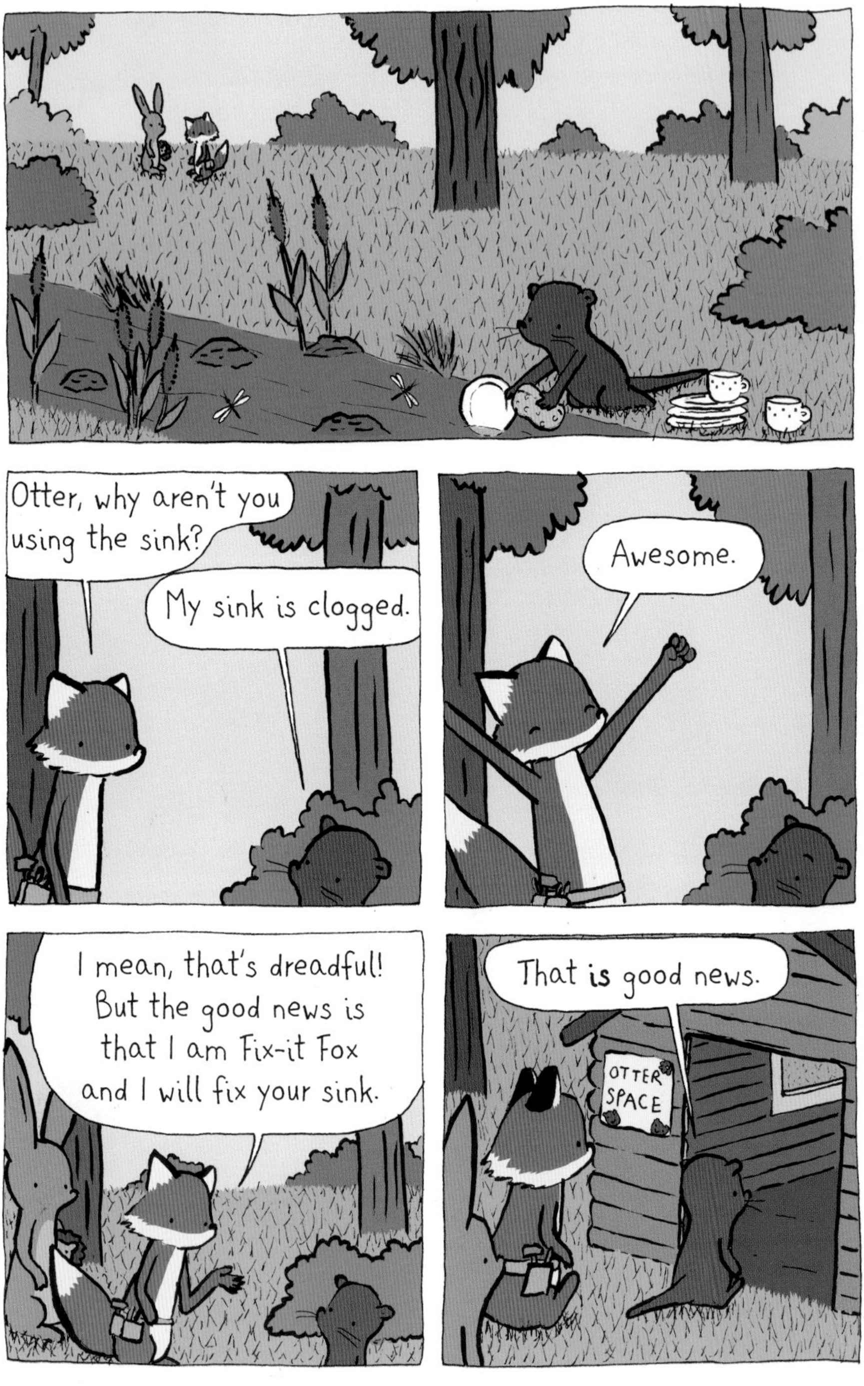
Otter, why aren't you using the sink?
My sink is clogged.
Awesome.
I mean, that's dreadful! But the good news is that I am Fix-it Fox and I will fix your sink.
That is good news.
OTTER SPACE

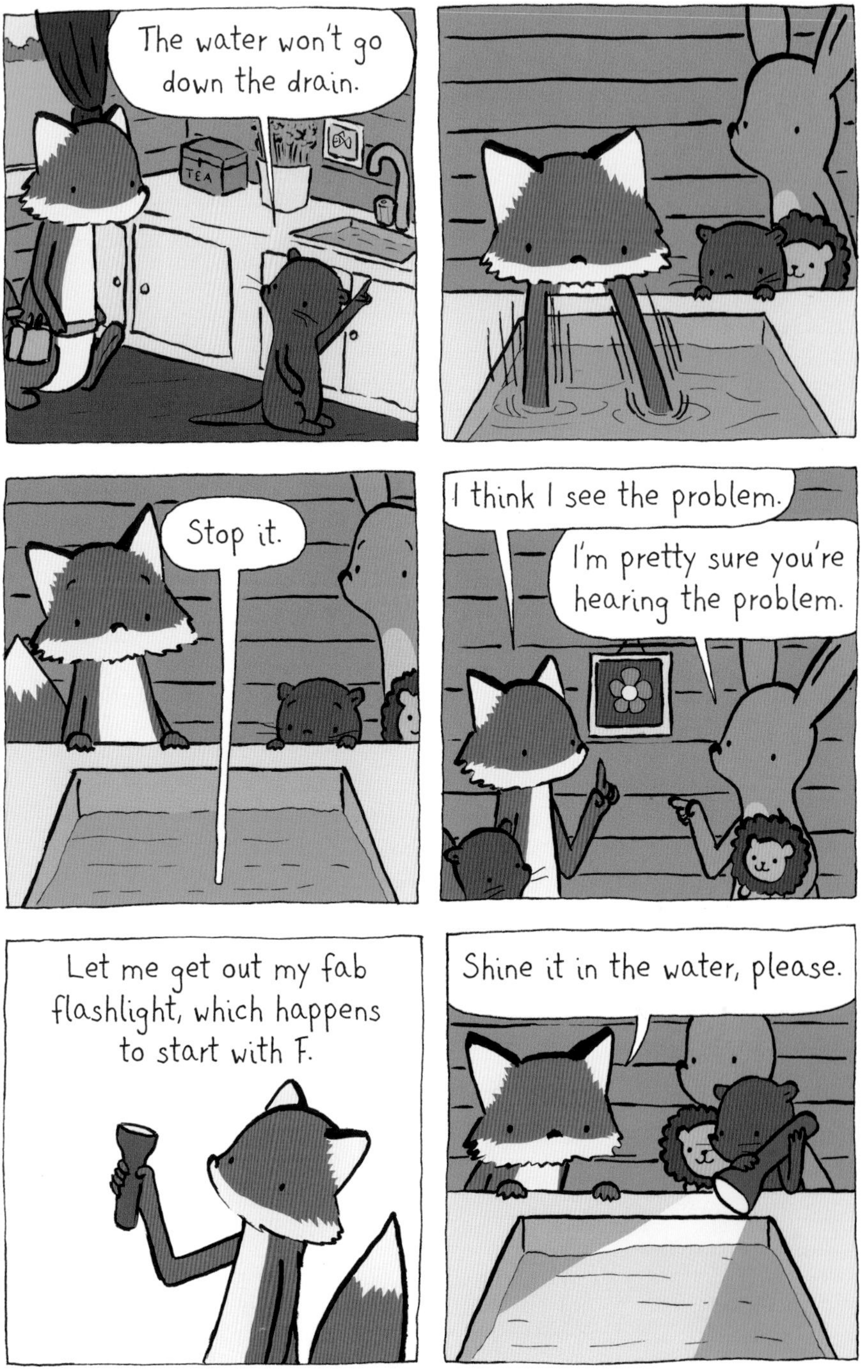
The water won't go down the drain.
Stop it.
I think I see the problem.
I'm pretty sure you're hearing the problem.
Let me get out my fab flashlight, which happens to start with F.
Shine it in the water, please.

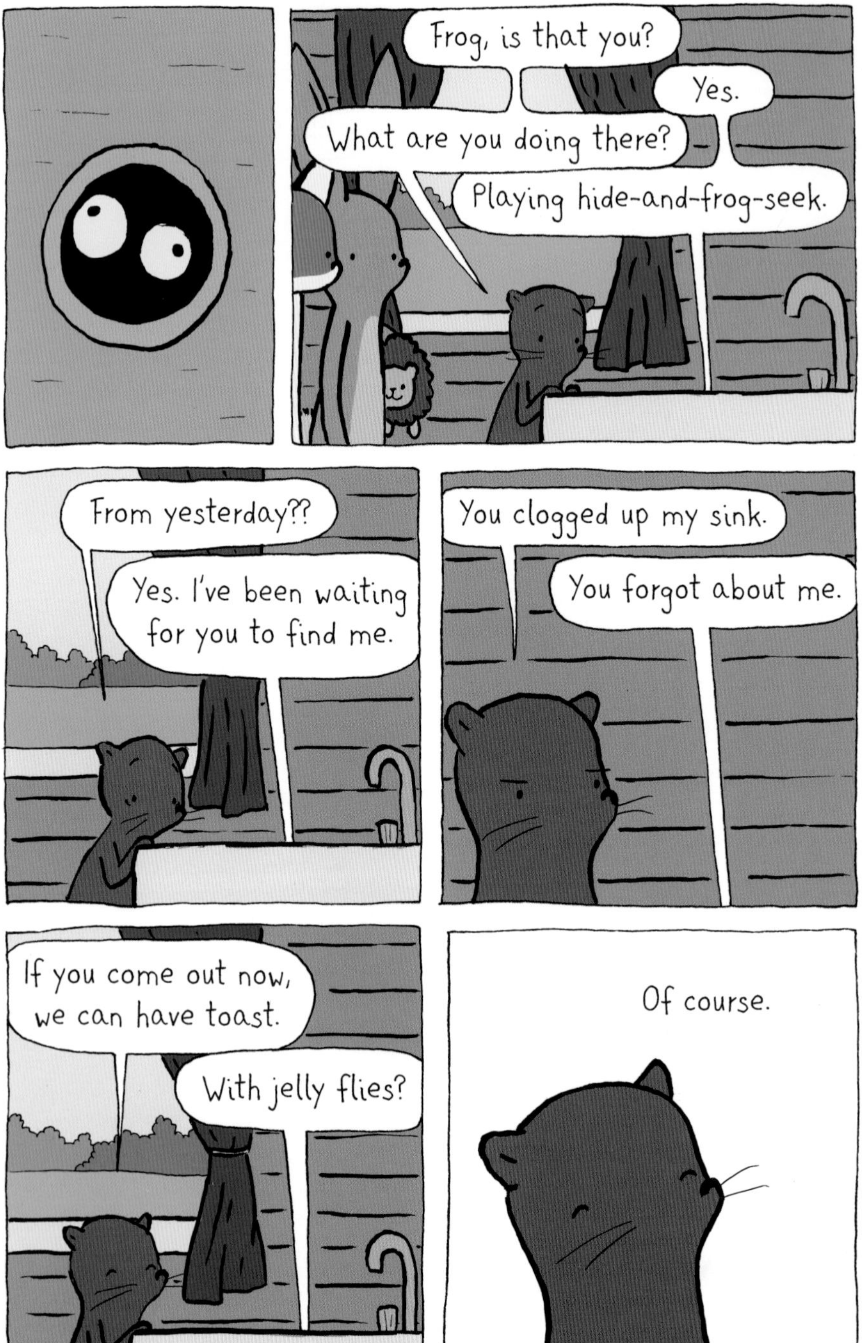
Frog, is that you?
Yes.
What are you doing there?
Playing hide-and-frog-seek.
From yesterday??
Yes. I've been waiting for you to find me.
You clogged up my sink.
You forgot about me.
If you come out now, we can have toast.
With jelly flies?
Of course.

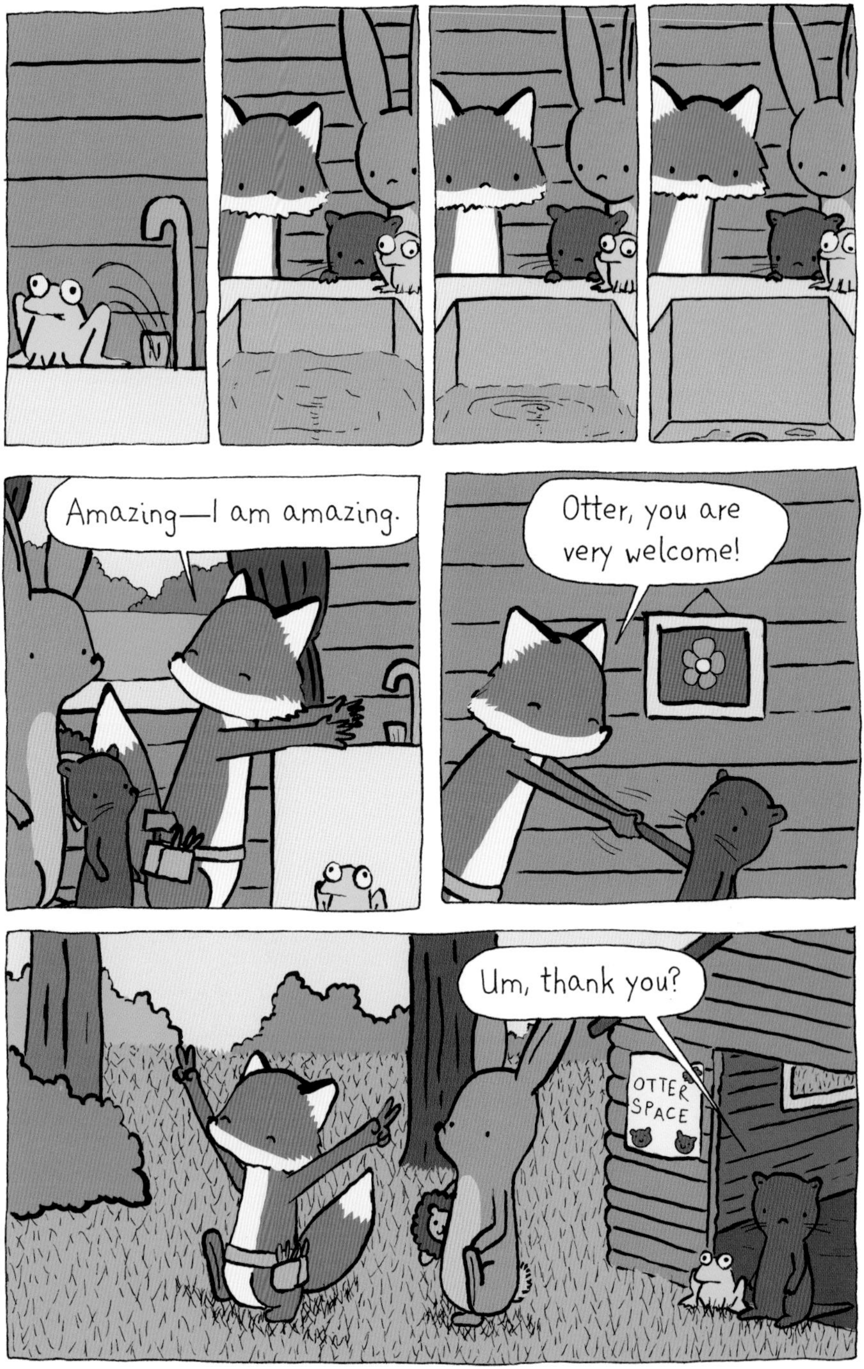
Amazing—I am amazing.
Otter, you are very welcome!
Um, thank you?
OTTER SPACE

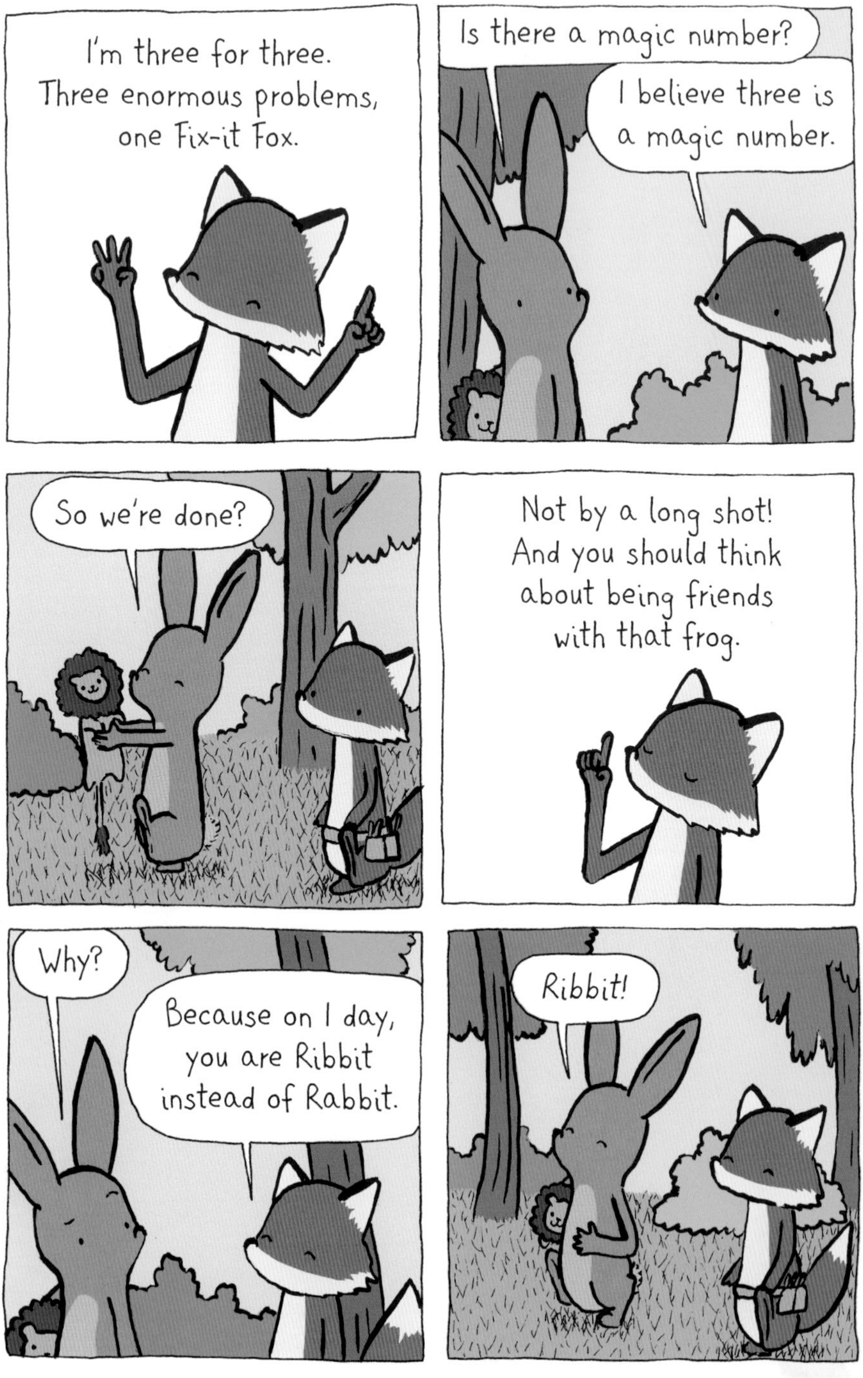
I'm three for three. Three enormous problems, one Fix-it Fox.
Is there a magic number?
I believe three is a magic number.
So we're done?
Not by a long shot! And you should think about being friends with that frog.
Why?
Because on 1 day, you are Ribbit instead of Rabbit.
Ribbit!

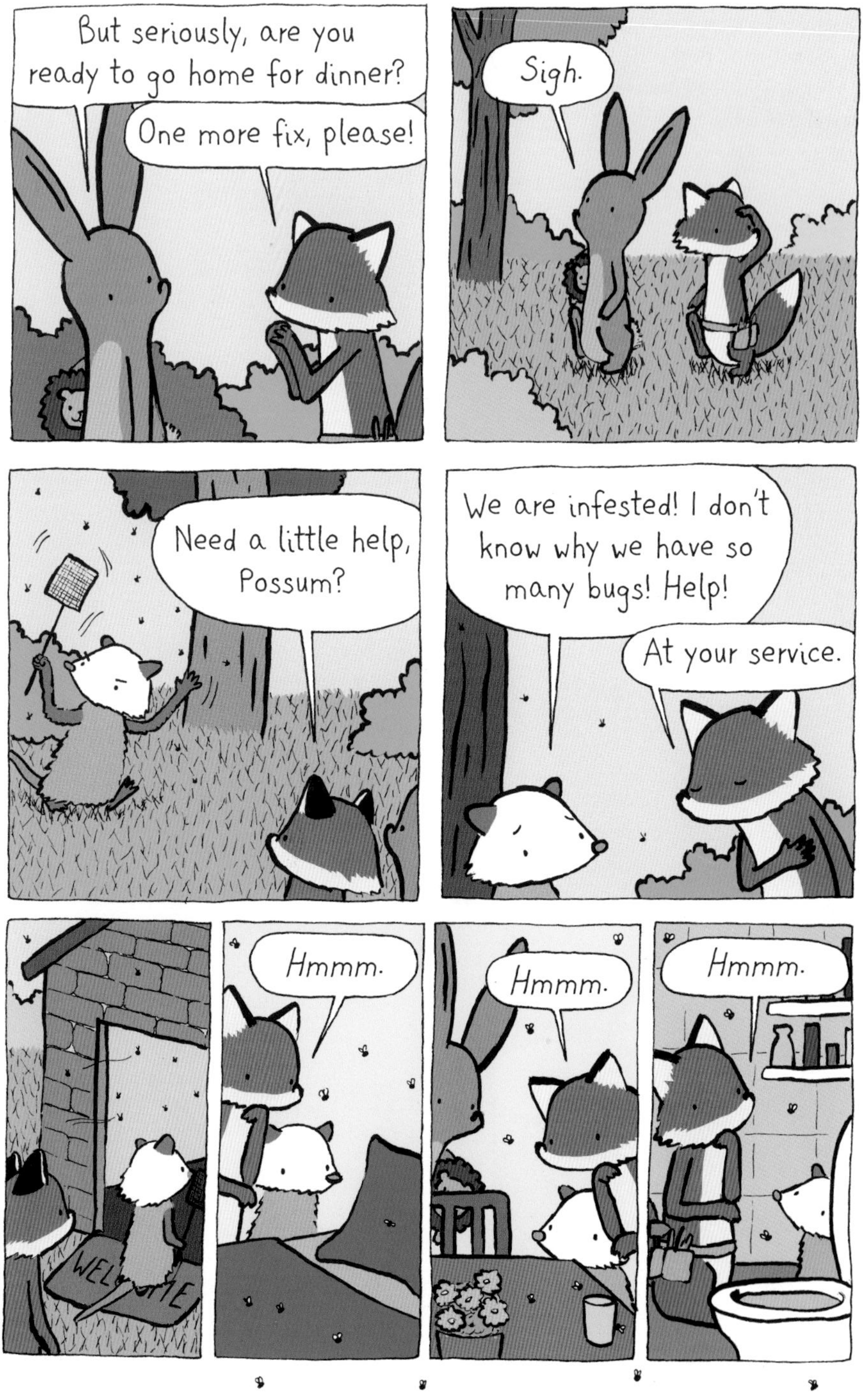
But seriously, are you ready to go home for dinner?
One more fix, please!
Sigh.
Need a little help, Possum?
We are infested! I don't know why we have so many bugs! Help!
At your service.
WELCOME
Hmmm.
Hmmm.
Hmmm.

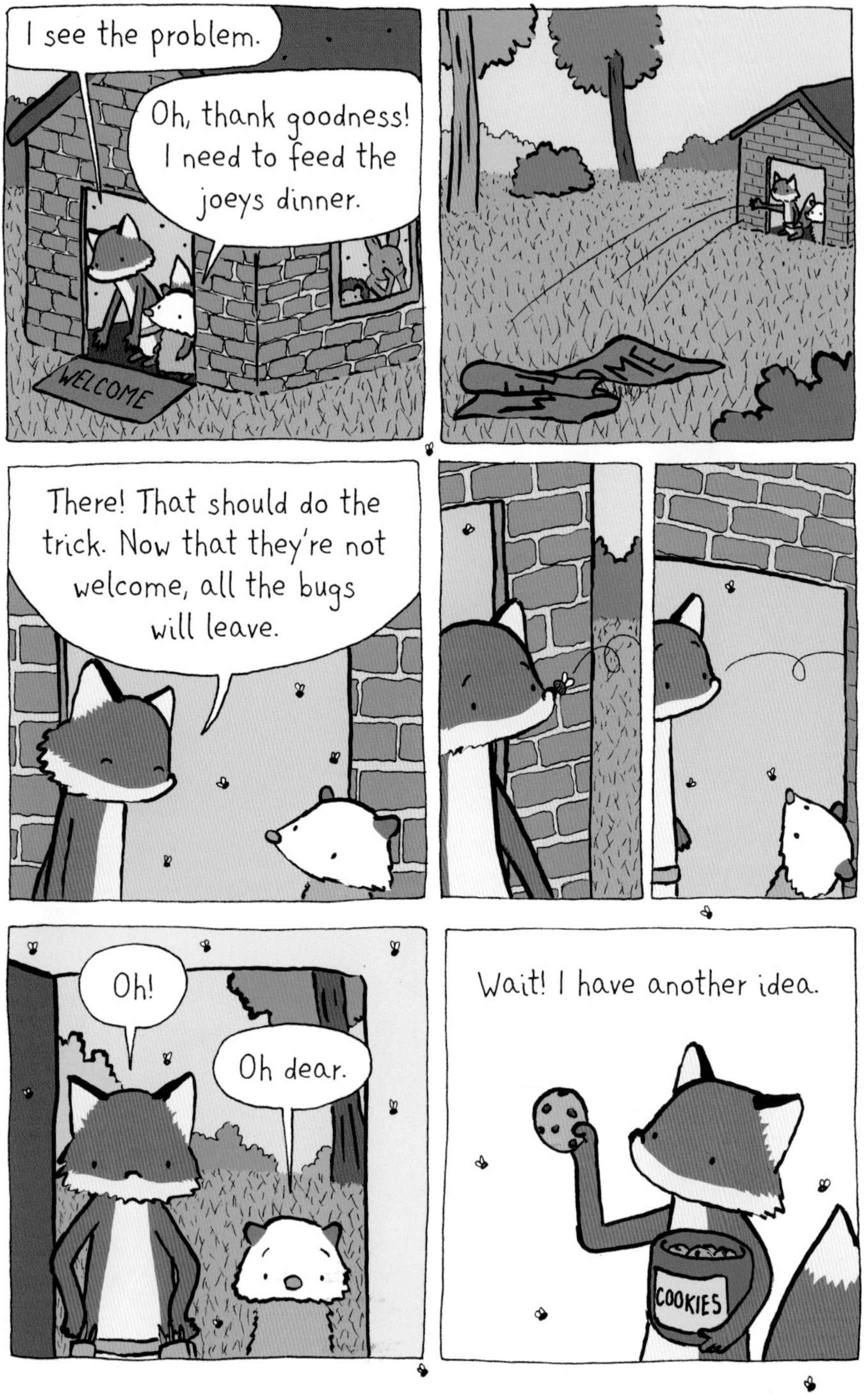
I see the problem.
Oh, thank goodness! I need to feed the joeys dinner.
WELCOME
There! That should do the trick. Now that they're not welcome, all the bugs will leave.
Oh!
Oh dear.
Wait! I have another idea.
COOKIES

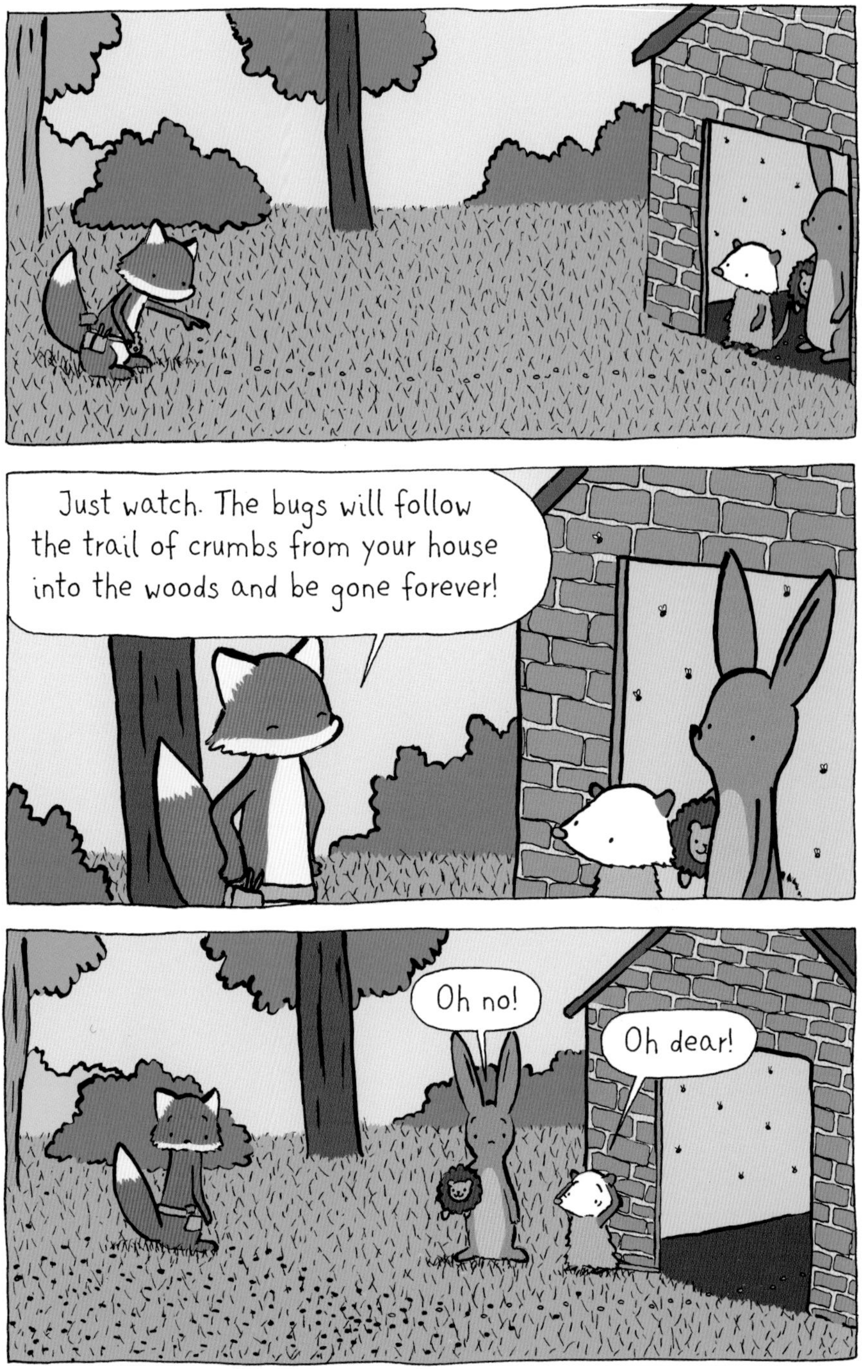
Just watch. The bugs will follow the trail of crumbs from your house into the woods and be gone forever!
Oh no!
Oh dear!

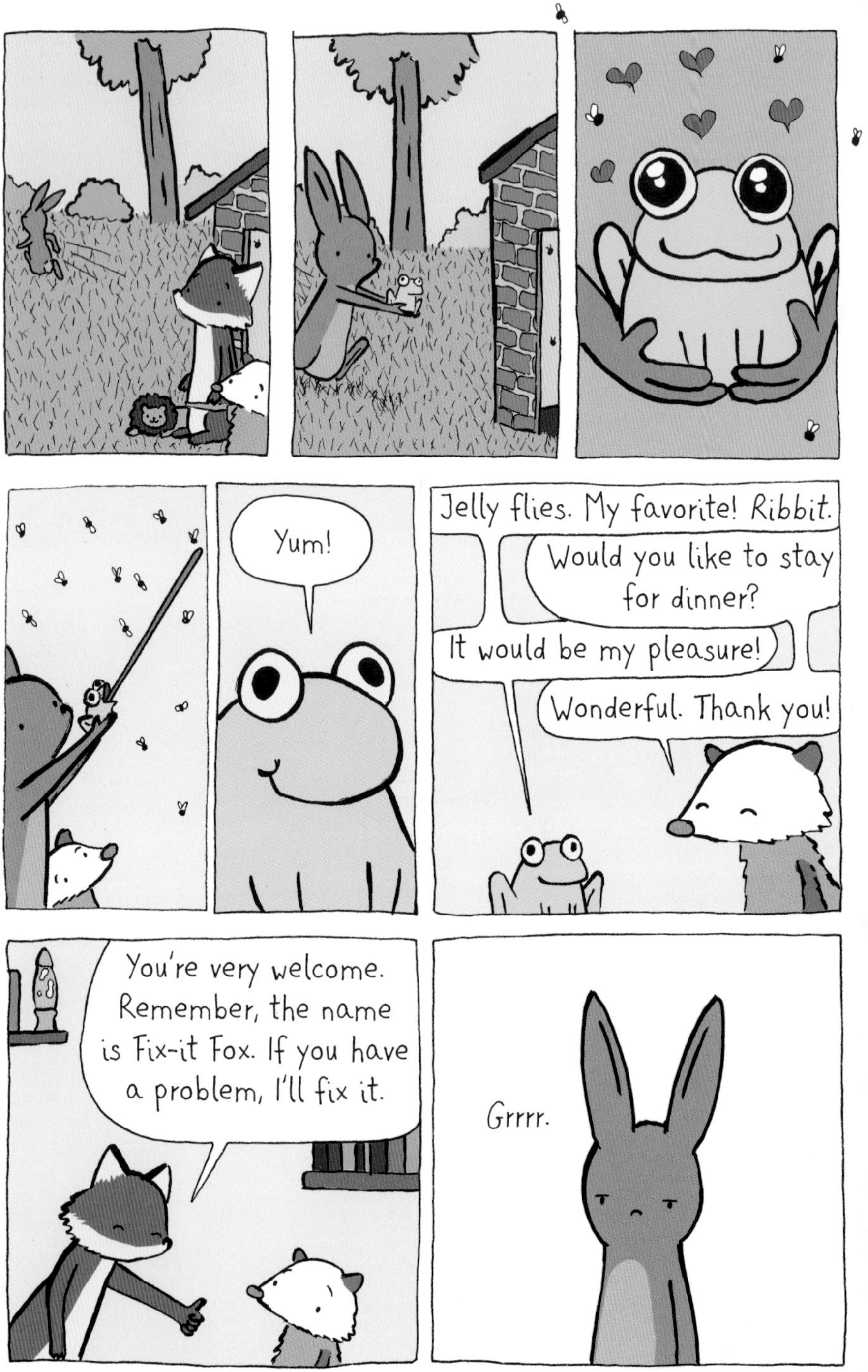
Yum!
Jelly flies. My favorite! *Ribbit.*
Would you like to stay for dinner?
It would be my pleasure!
Wonderful. Thank you!
You're very welcome. Remember, the name is Fix-it Fox. If you have a problem, I'll fix it.
Grrrr.

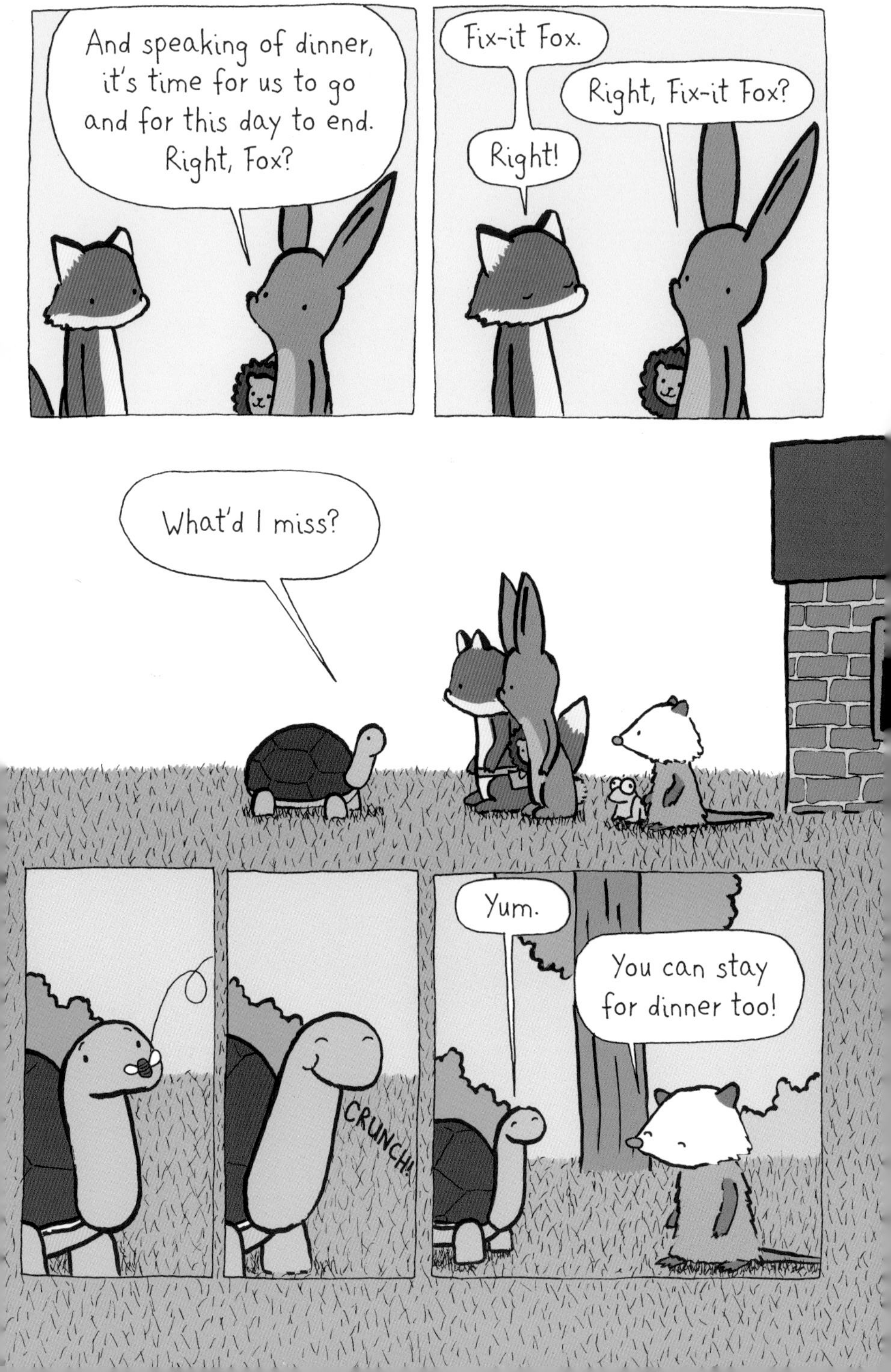

And speaking of dinner, it's time for us to go and for this day to end. Right, Fox?
Fix-it Fox.
Right!
Right, Fix-it Fox?
What'd I miss?
CRUNCH!
Yum.
You can stay for dinner too!

STORY TWO

PARTY, PIZZA & PLANS

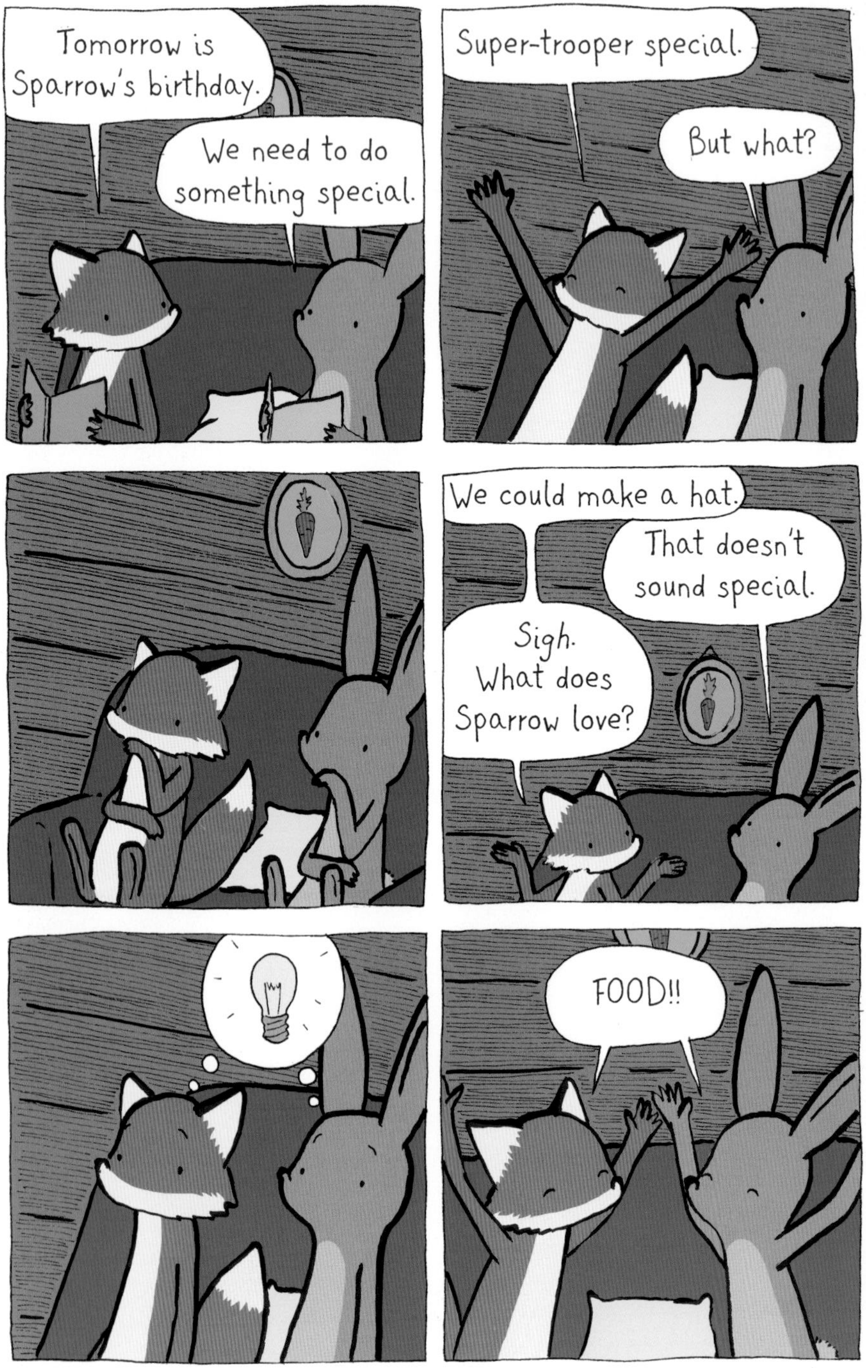
Tomorrow is Sparrow's birthday.
We need to do something special.
Super-trooper special.
But what?
We could make a hat.
That doesn't sound special.
Sigh. What does Sparrow love?
FOOD!!

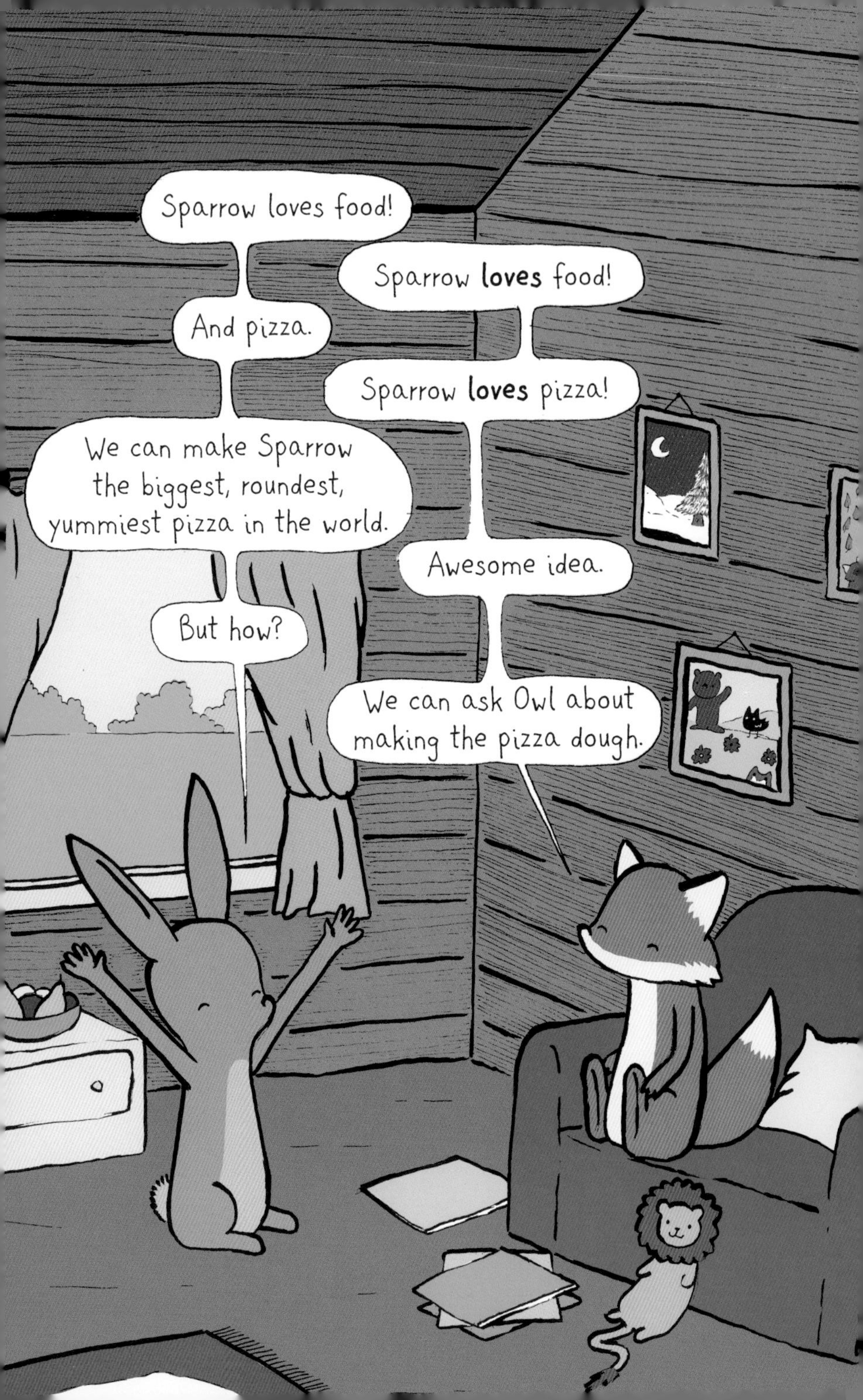
Sparrow loves food!
Sparrow **loves** food!
And pizza.
Sparrow **loves** pizza!
We can make Sparrow the biggest, roundest, yummiest pizza in the world.
Awesome idea.
But how?
We can ask Owl about making the pizza dough.

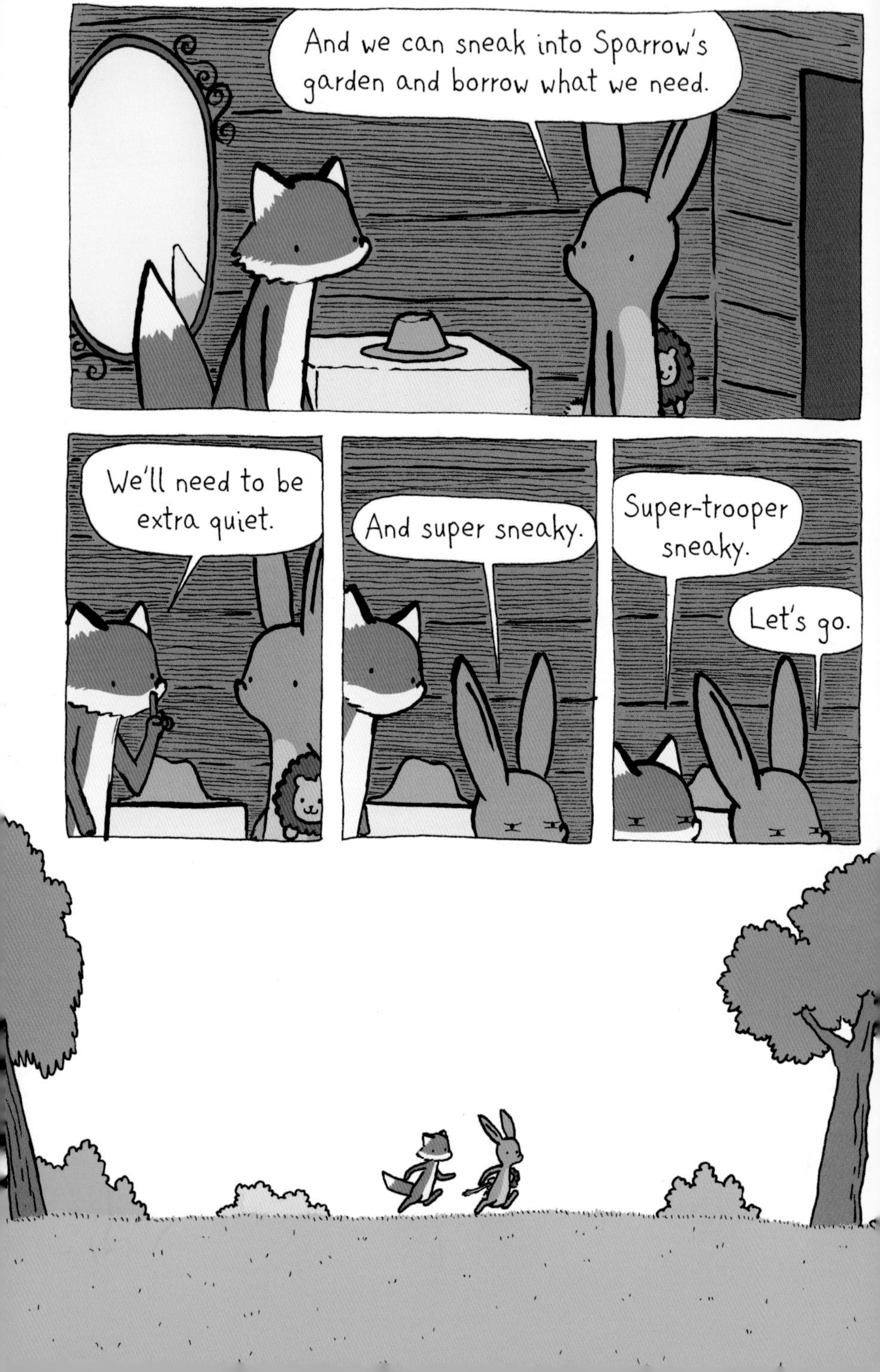
And we can sneak into Sparrow's garden and borrow what we need.
We'll need to be extra quiet.
And super sneaky.
Super-trooper sneaky.
Let's go.

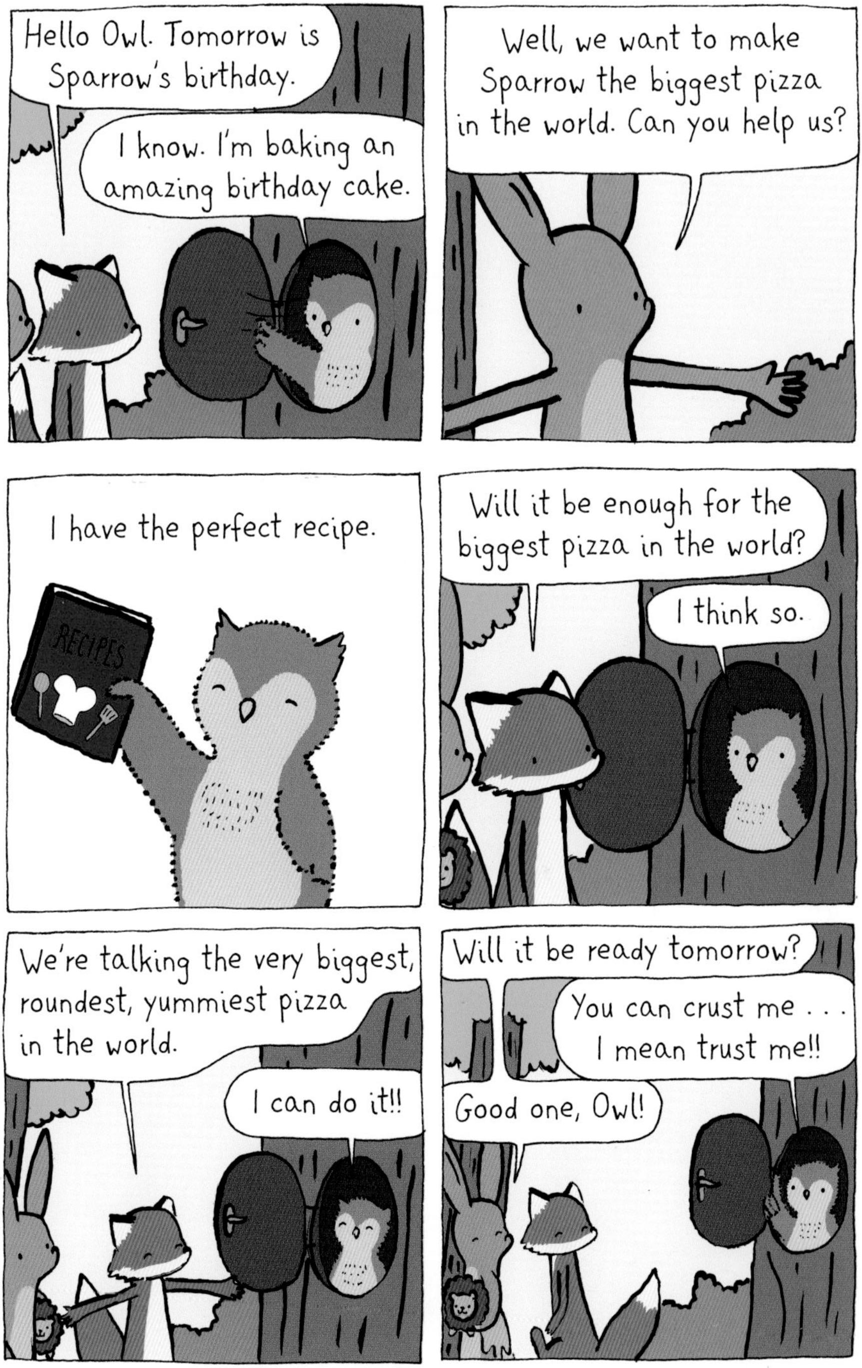
Hello Owl. Tomorrow is Sparrow's birthday.
I know. I'm baking an amazing birthday cake.
Well, we want to make Sparrow the biggest pizza in the world. Can you help us?
I have the perfect recipe.
RECIPES
Will it be enough for the biggest pizza in the world?
I think so.
We're talking the very biggest, roundest, yummiest pizza in the world.
I can do it!!
Will it be ready tomorrow?
You can crust me . . . I mean trust me!!
Good one, Owl!

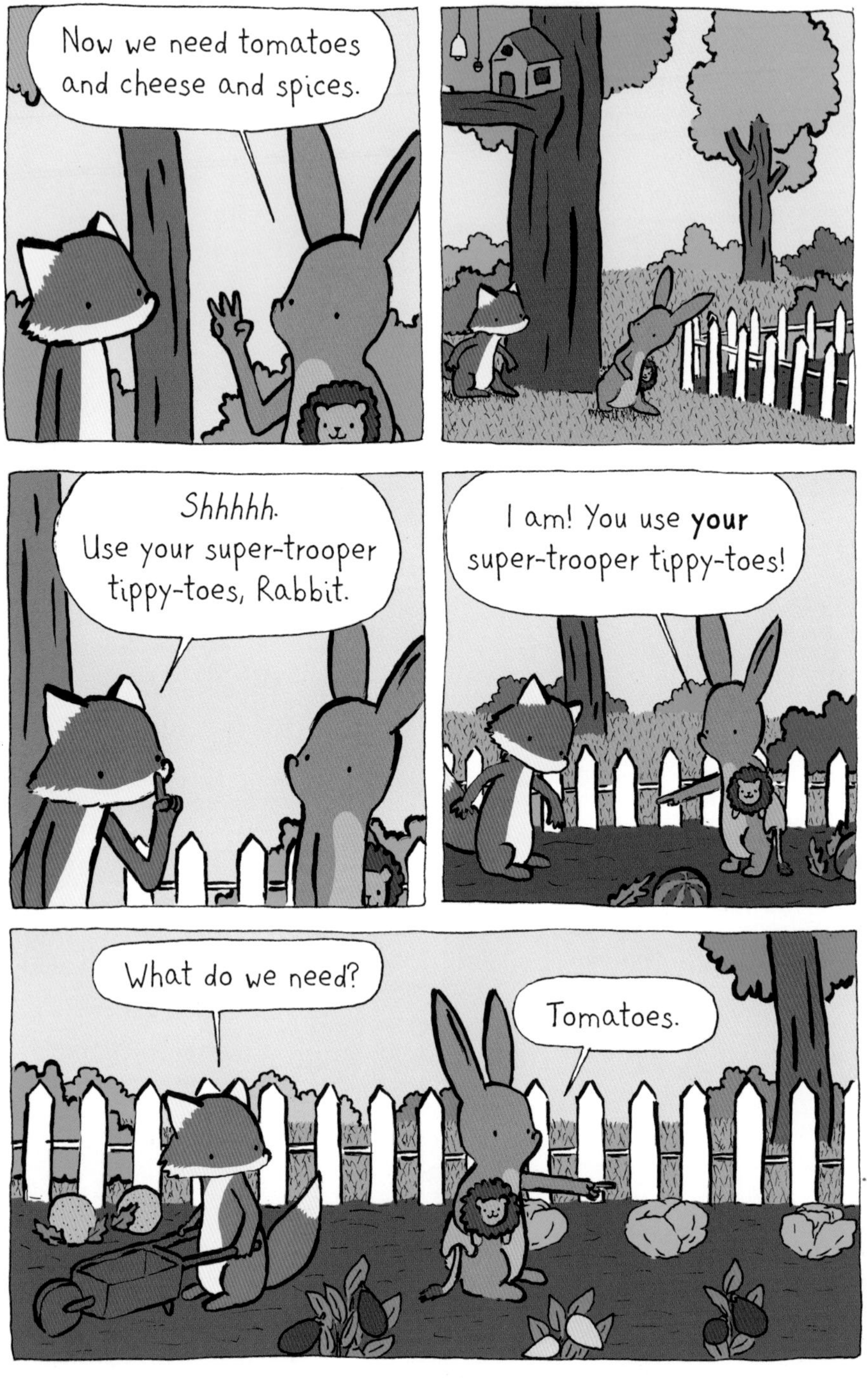
Now we need tomatoes and cheese and spices.
Shhhhh. Use your super-trooper tippy-toes, Rabbit.
I am! You use **your** super-trooper tippy-toes!
What do we need?
Tomatoes.

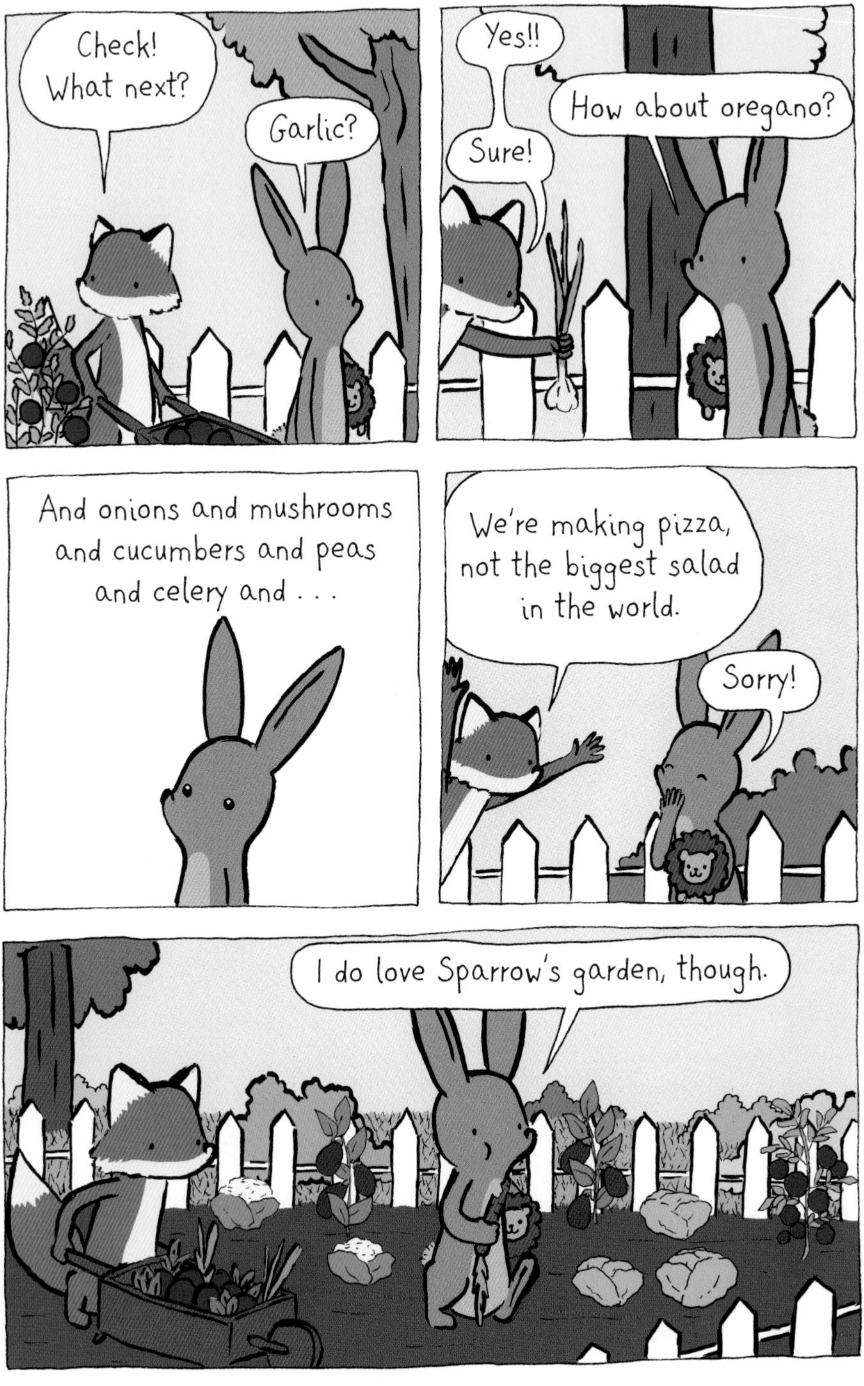
Check! What next?
Garlic?
Yes!!
Sure!
How about oregano?
And onions and mushrooms and cucumbers and peas and celery and . . .
We're making pizza, not the biggest salad in the world.
Sorry!
I do love Sparrow's garden, though.

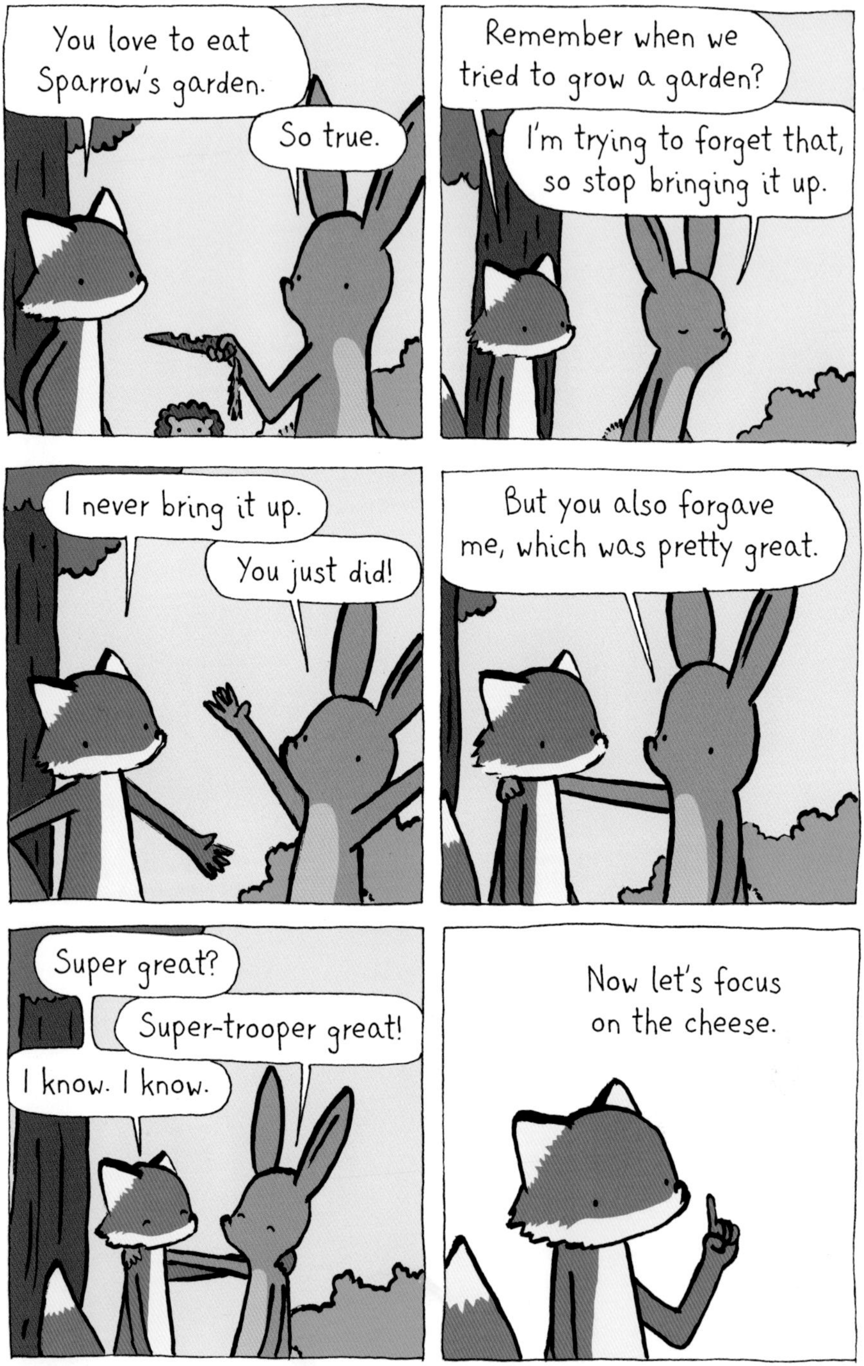
You love to eat Sparrow's garden.
So true.
Remember when we tried to grow a garden?
I'm trying to forget that, so stop bringing it up.
I never bring it up.
You just did!
But you also forgave me, which was pretty great.
Super great?
Super-trooper great!
I know. I know.
Now let's focus on the cheese.

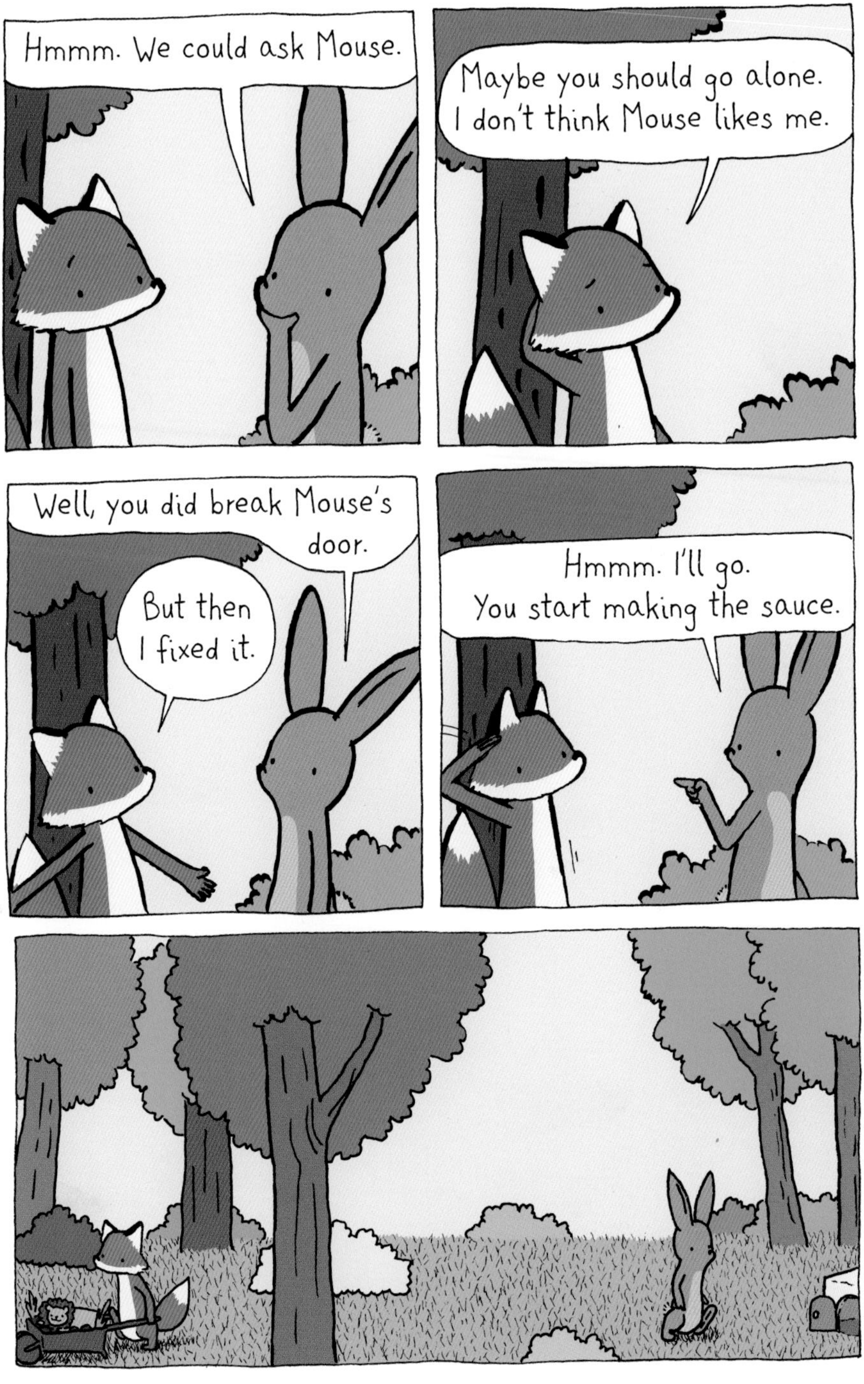
Hmmm. We could ask Mouse.
Maybe you should go alone. I don't think Mouse likes me.
Well, you did break Mouse's door.
But then I fixed it.
Hmmm. I'll go. You start making the sauce.

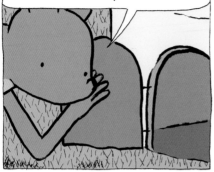
Hello, Mouse. I'm wondering if I could ask you a favor.

Hello!! I never got the chance to thank Fox. Ever since Fox "fixed" my door, I began leaving it open. I've made so many new friends.

Wow! That's . . . surprising.

Isn't it wonderful? Now, how can I help you?

Well, we need cheese. Lots of cheese.

Follow me.

Chamber of Cheese

34

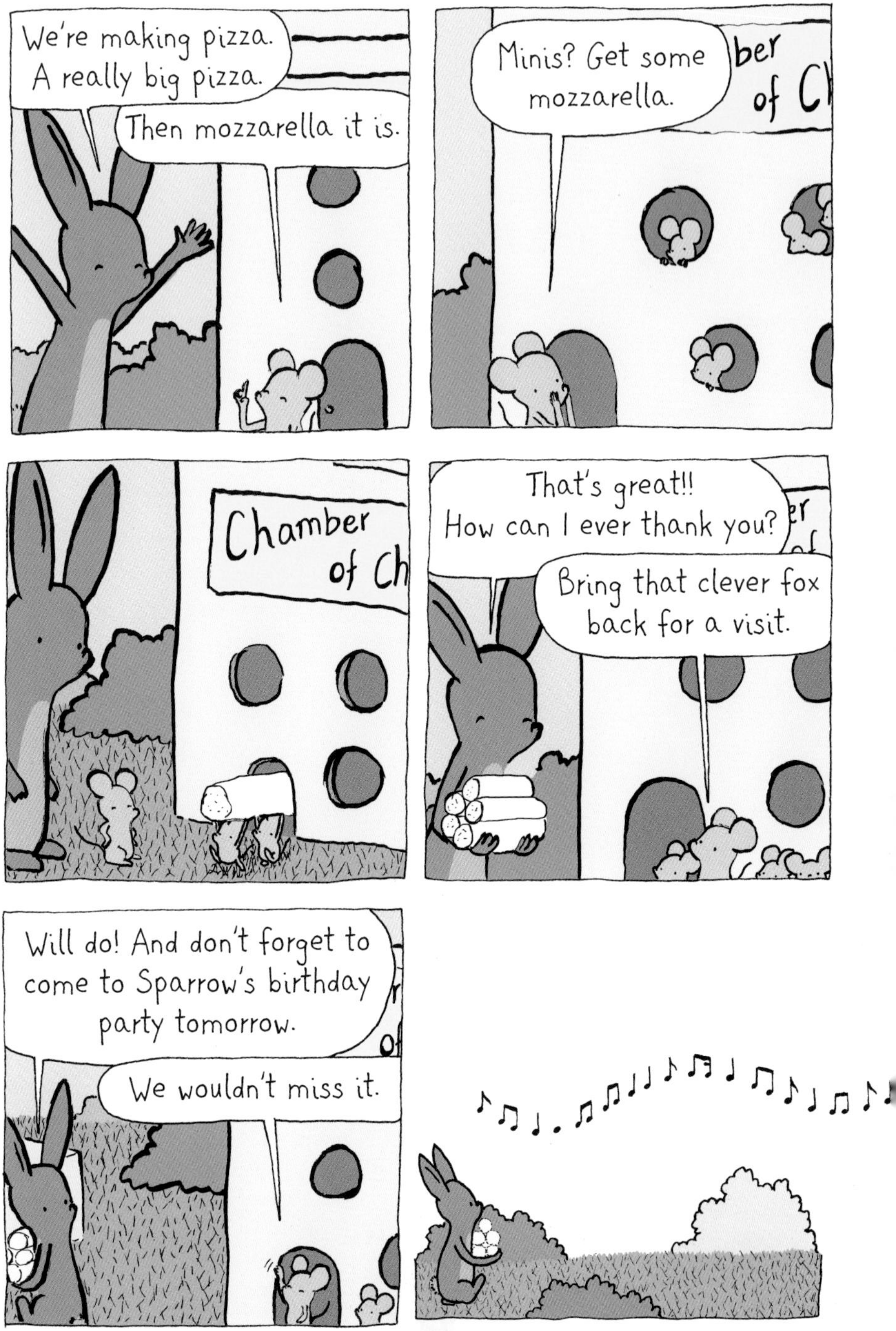
We're making pizza. A really big pizza.
Then mozzarella it is.
Minis? Get some mozzarella.
ber of Ch
Chamber of Ch
That's great!! How can I ever thank you?
Bring that clever fox back for a visit.
Will do! And don't forget to come to Sparrow's birthday party tomorrow.
We wouldn't miss it.

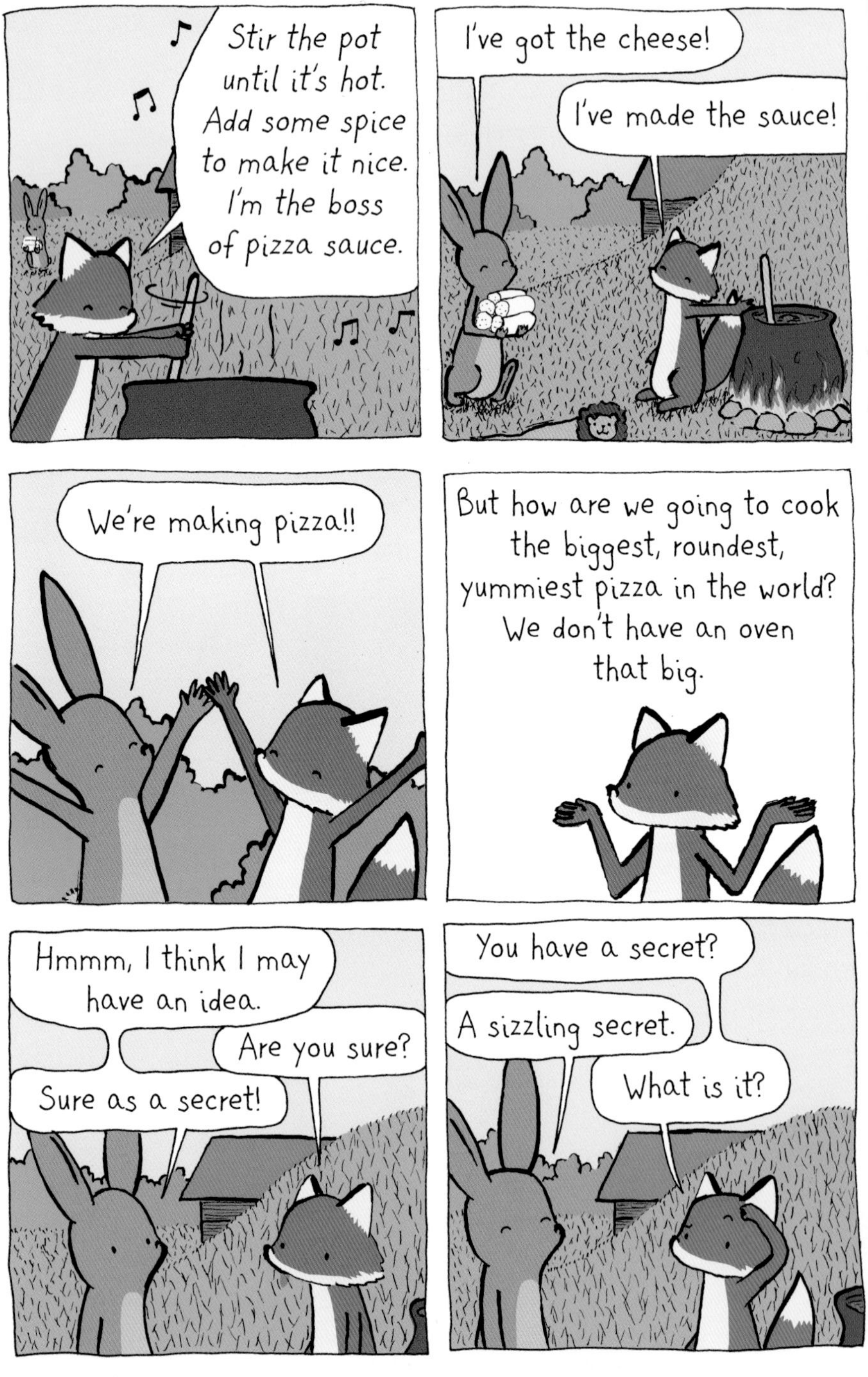

Stir the pot until it's hot. Add some spice to make it nice. I'm the boss of pizza sauce.
I've got the cheese!
I've made the sauce!
We're making pizza!!
But how are we going to cook the biggest, roundest, yummiest pizza in the world? We don't have an oven that big.
Hmmm, I think I may have an idea.
Are you sure?
Sure as a secret!
You have a secret?
A sizzling secret.
What is it?

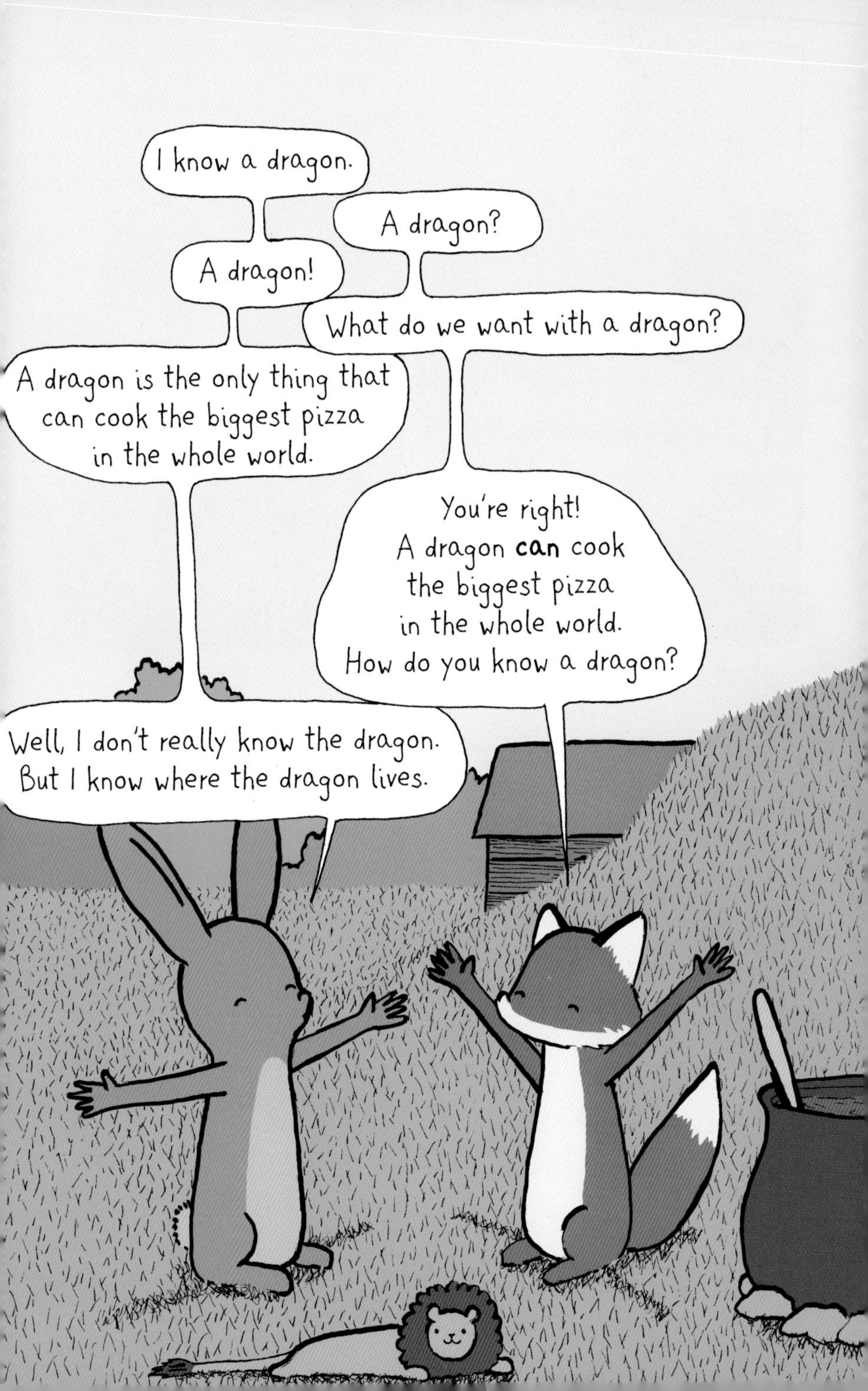
I know a dragon.
A dragon?
A dragon!
What do we want with a dragon?
A dragon is the only thing that can cook the biggest pizza in the whole world.
You're right! A dragon **can** cook the biggest pizza in the whole world. How do you know a dragon?
Well, I don't really know the dragon. But I know where the dragon lives.

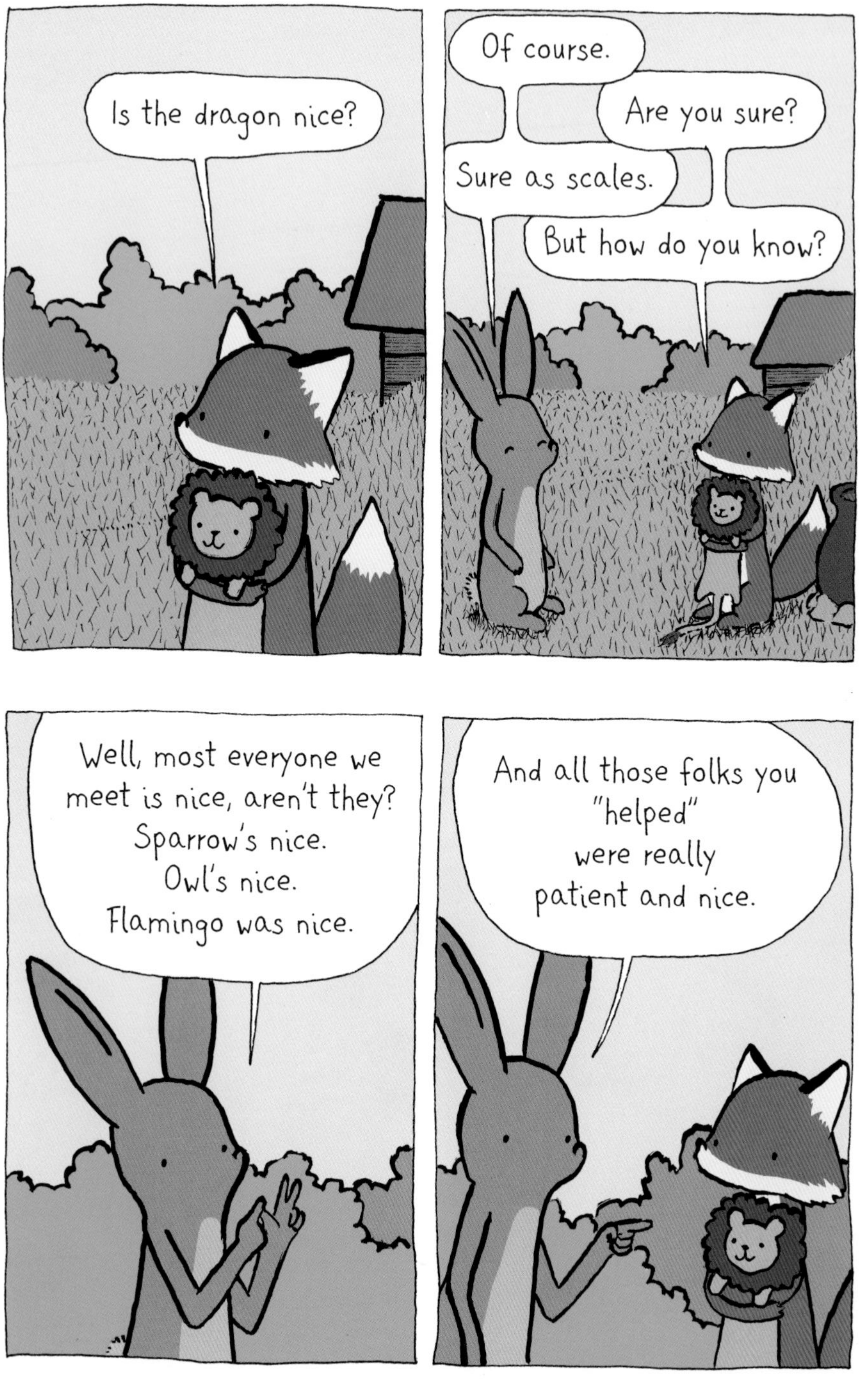
Is the dragon nice?
Of course.
Are you sure?
Sure as scales.
But how do you know?
Well, most everyone we meet is nice, aren't they? Sparrow's nice. Owl's nice. Flamingo was nice.
And all those folks you "helped" were really patient and nice.

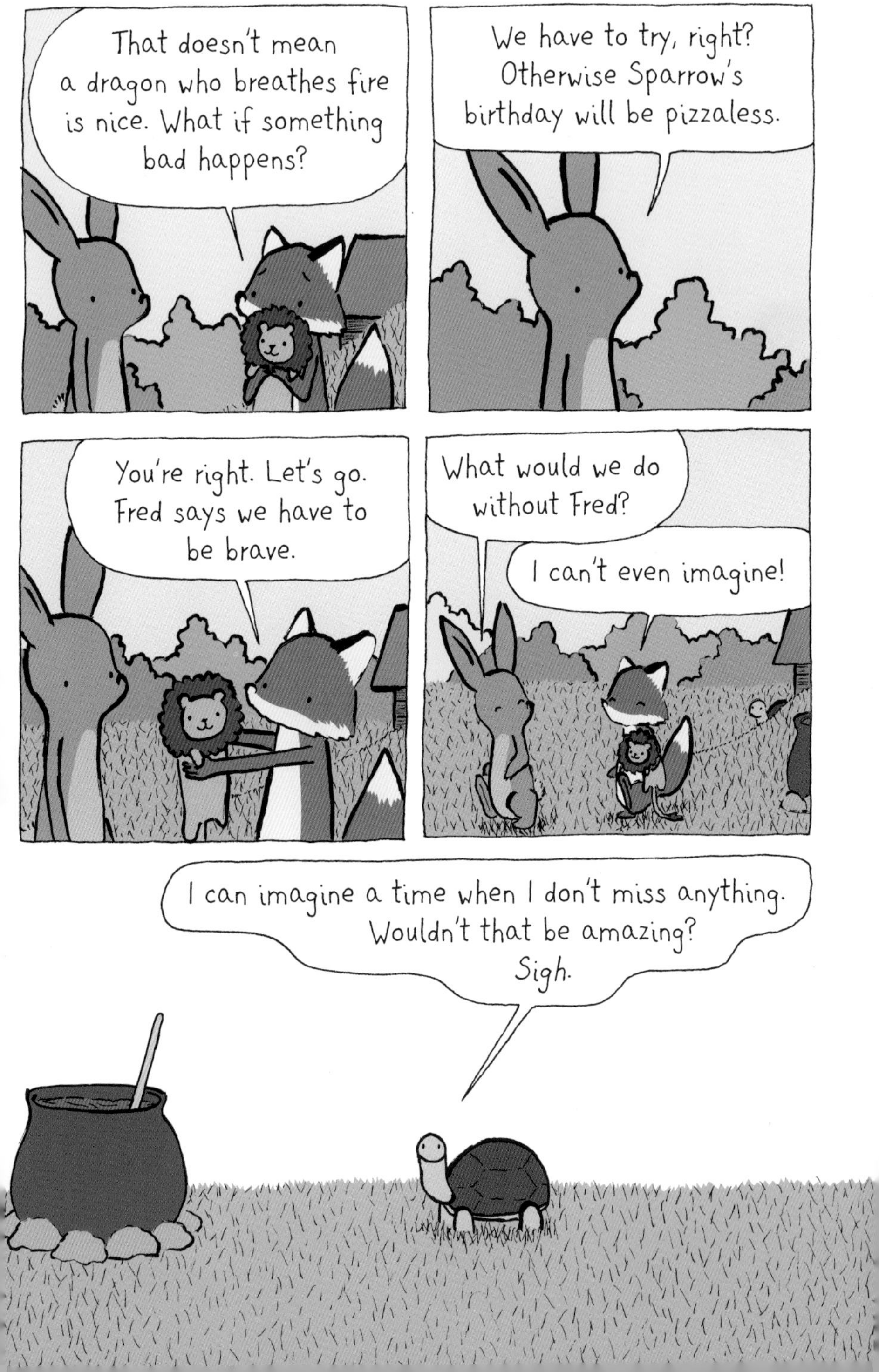
That doesn't mean a dragon who breathes fire is nice. What if something bad happens?
We have to try, right? Otherwise Sparrow's birthday will be pizzaless.
You're right. Let's go. Fred says we have to be brave.
What would we do without Fred?
I can't even imagine!
I can imagine a time when I don't miss anything. Wouldn't that be amazing? Sigh.

STORY THREE

DARING DRAGON DAYS

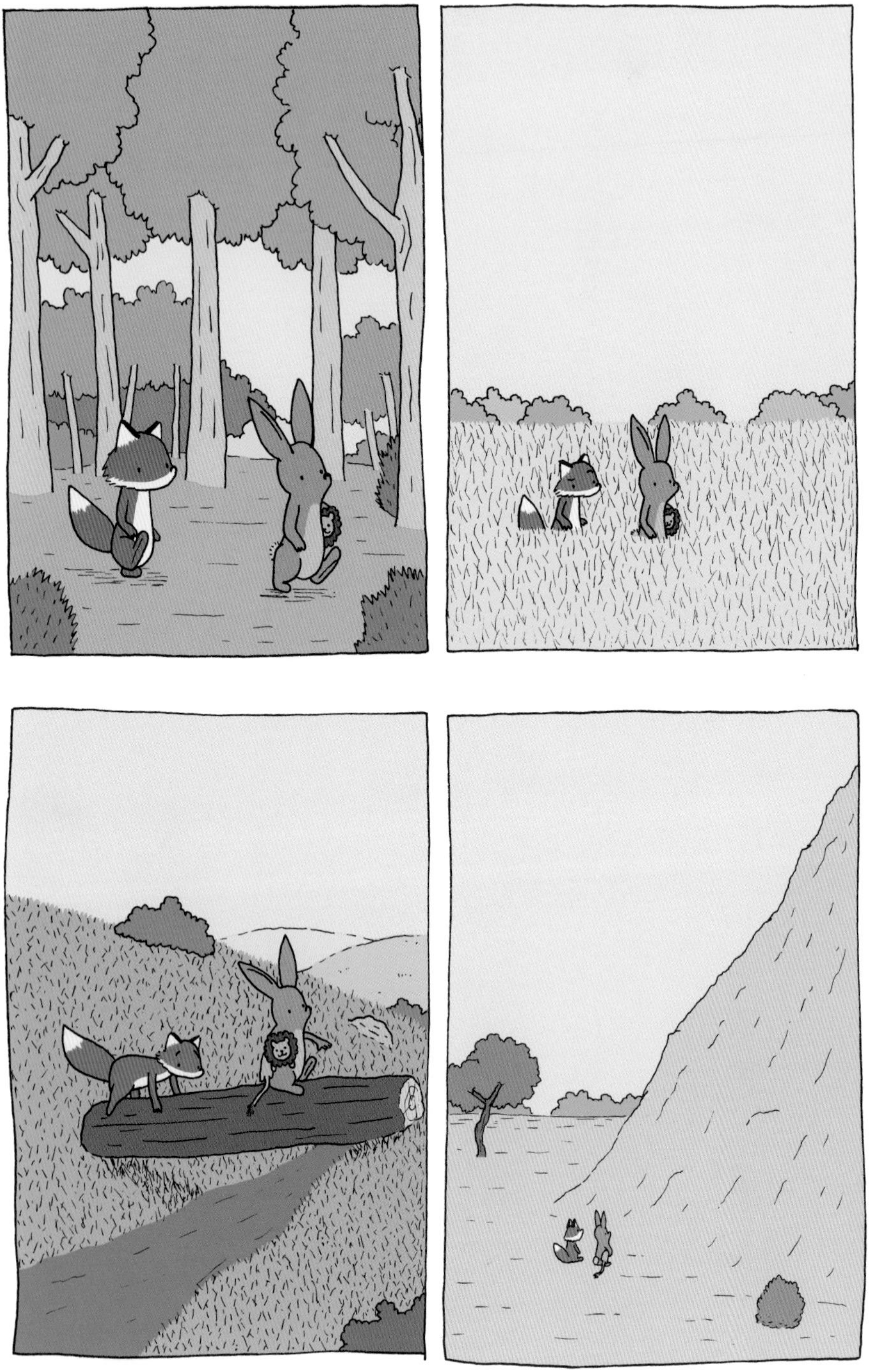

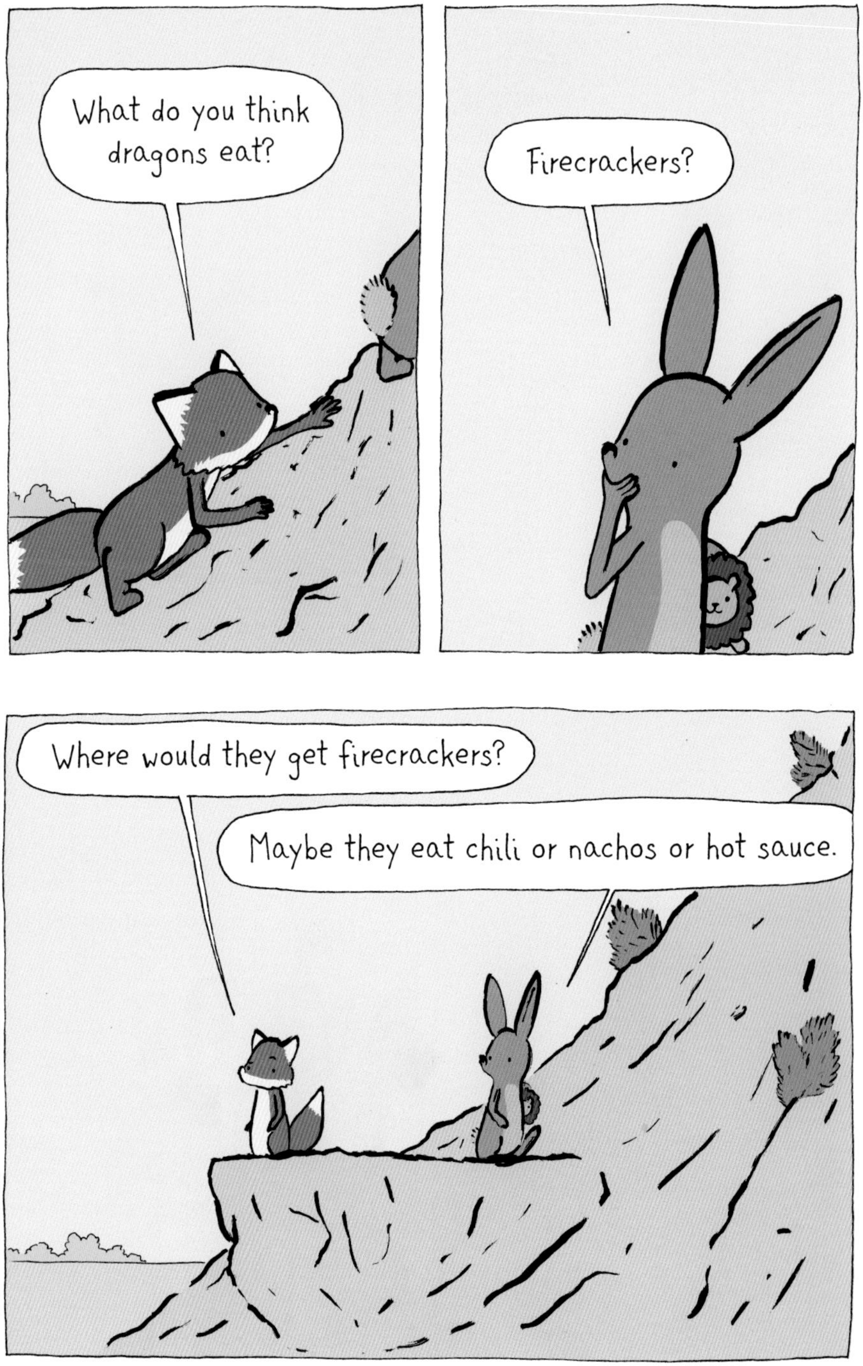
What do you think dragons eat?
Firecrackers?
Where would they get firecrackers?
Maybe they eat chili or nachos or hot sauce.

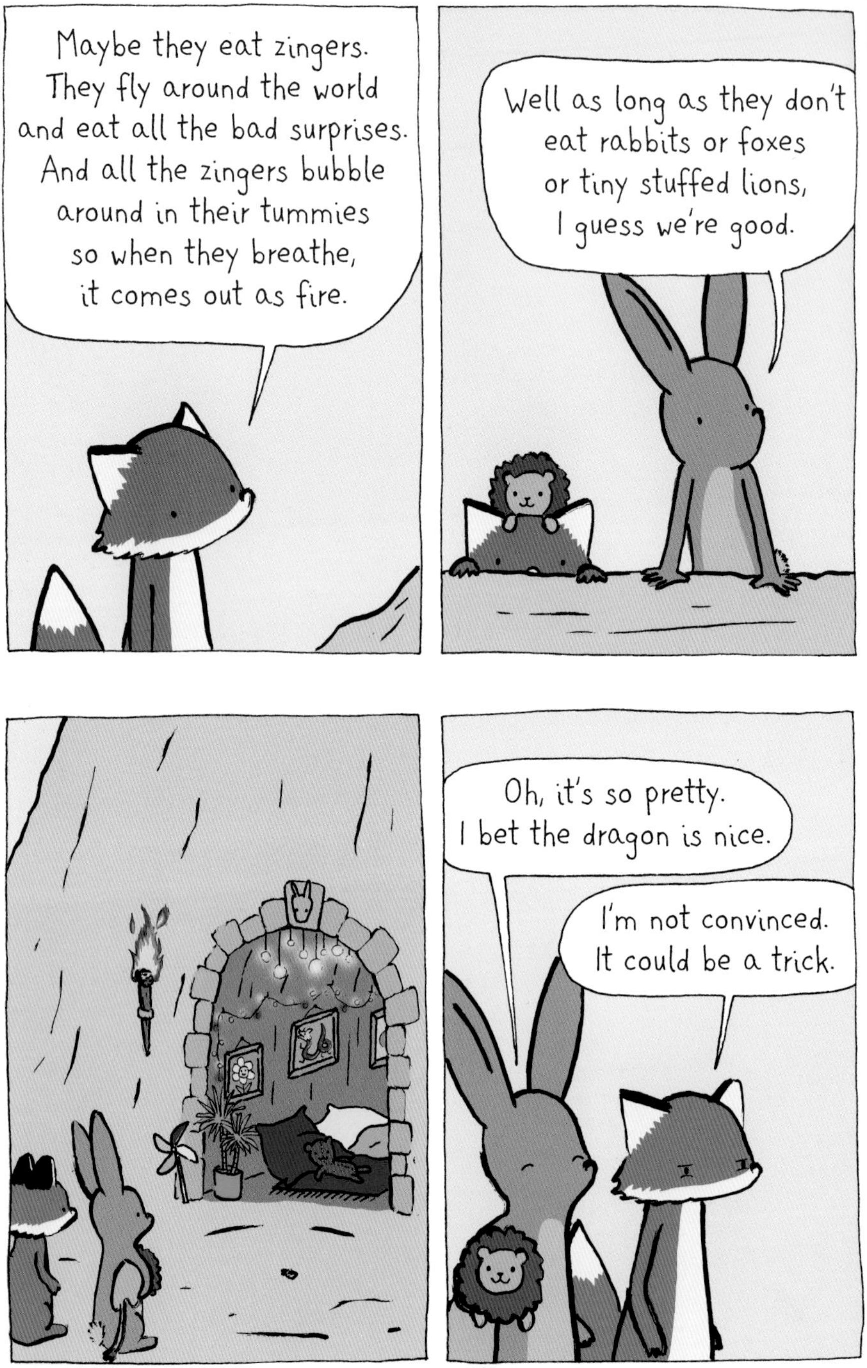
Maybe they eat zingers. They fly around the world and eat all the bad surprises. And all the zingers bubble around in their tummies so when they breathe, it comes out as fire.
Well as long as they don't eat rabbits or foxes or tiny stuffed lions, I guess we're good.
Oh, it's so pretty. I bet the dragon is nice.
I'm not convinced. It could be a trick.

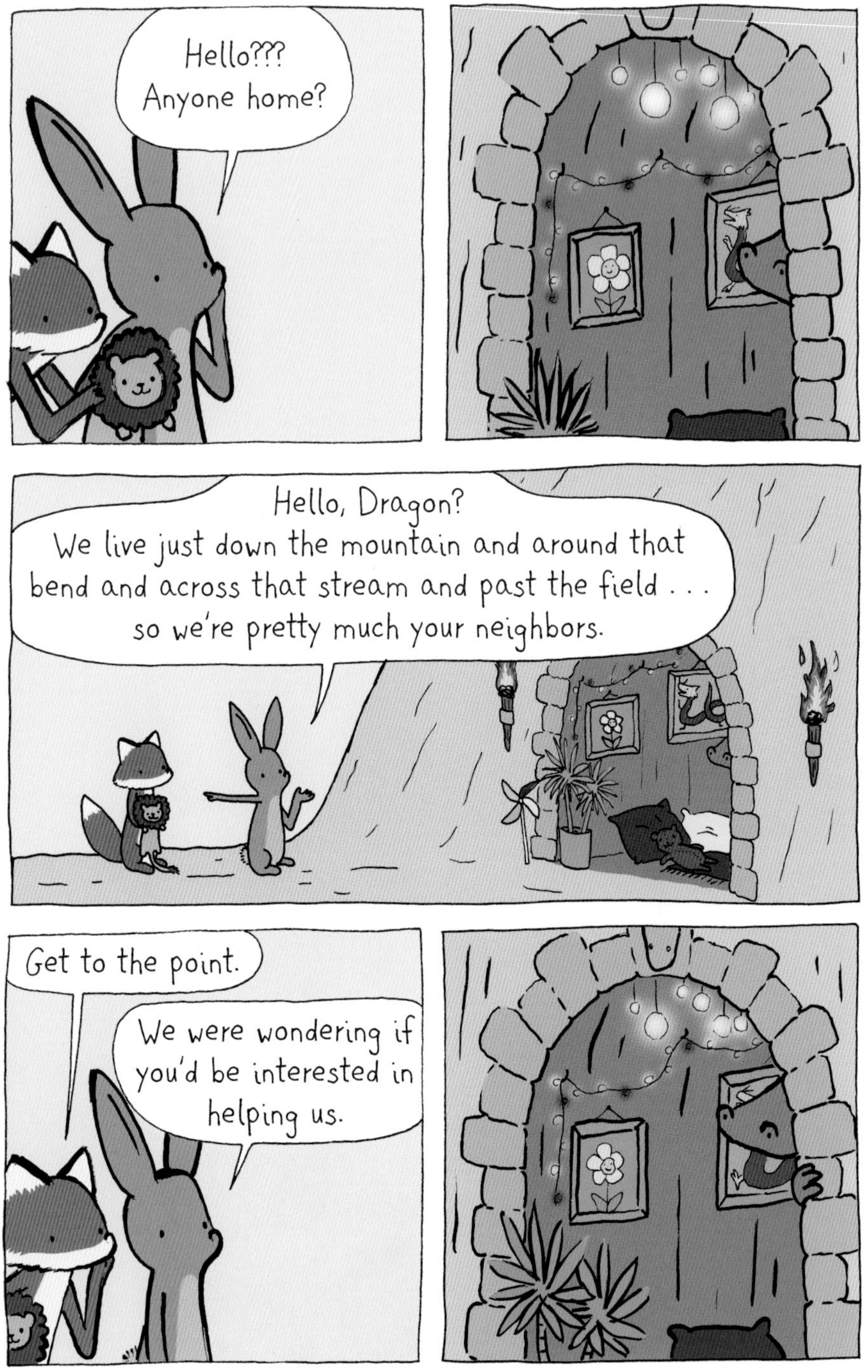
Hello???
Anyone home?
Hello, Dragon?
We live just down the mountain and around that bend and across that stream and past the field . . .
so we're pretty much your neighbors.
Get to the point.
We were wondering if you'd be interested in helping us.

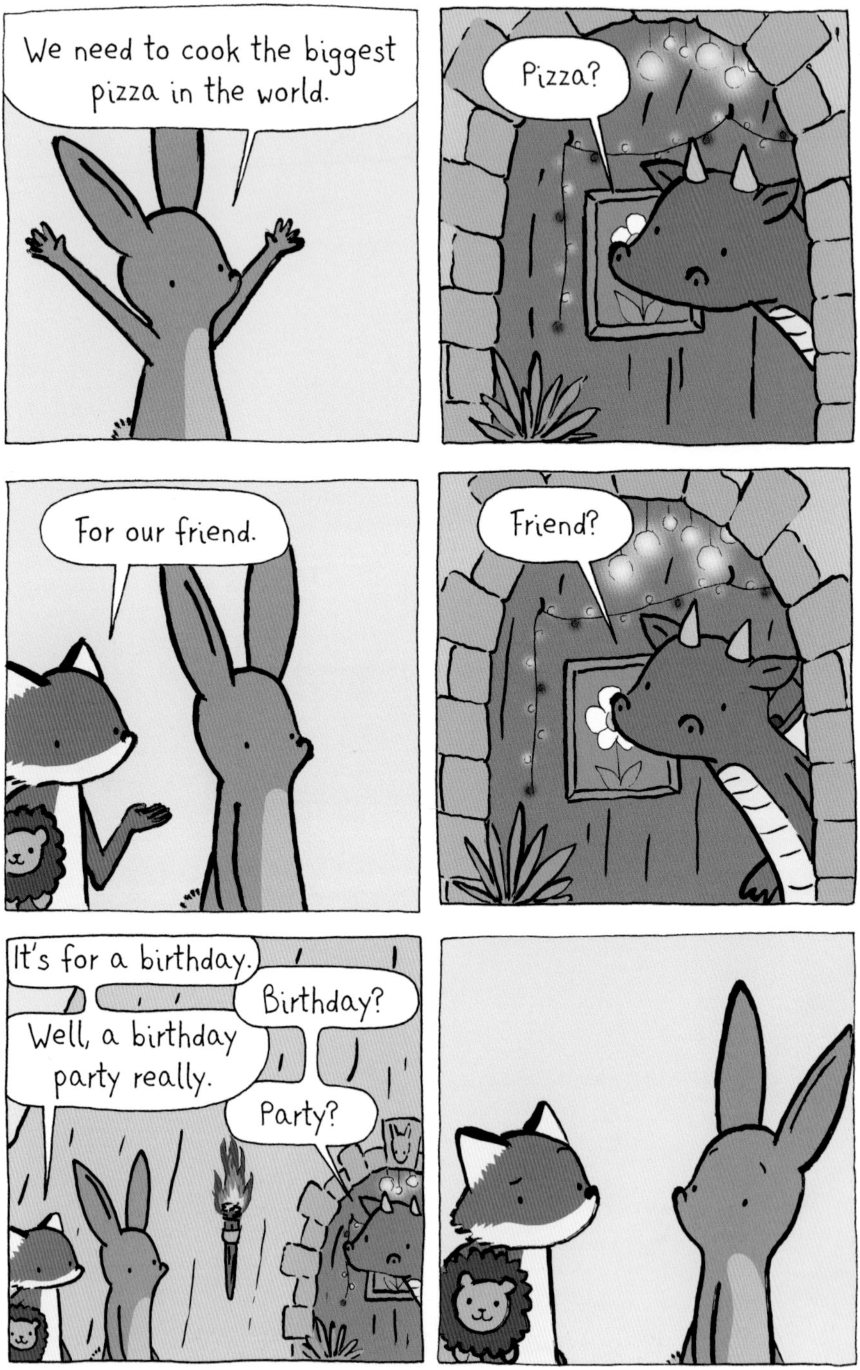
We need to cook the biggest pizza in the world.
Pizza?
For our friend.
Friend?
It's for a birthday.
Birthday?
Well, a birthday party really.
Party?

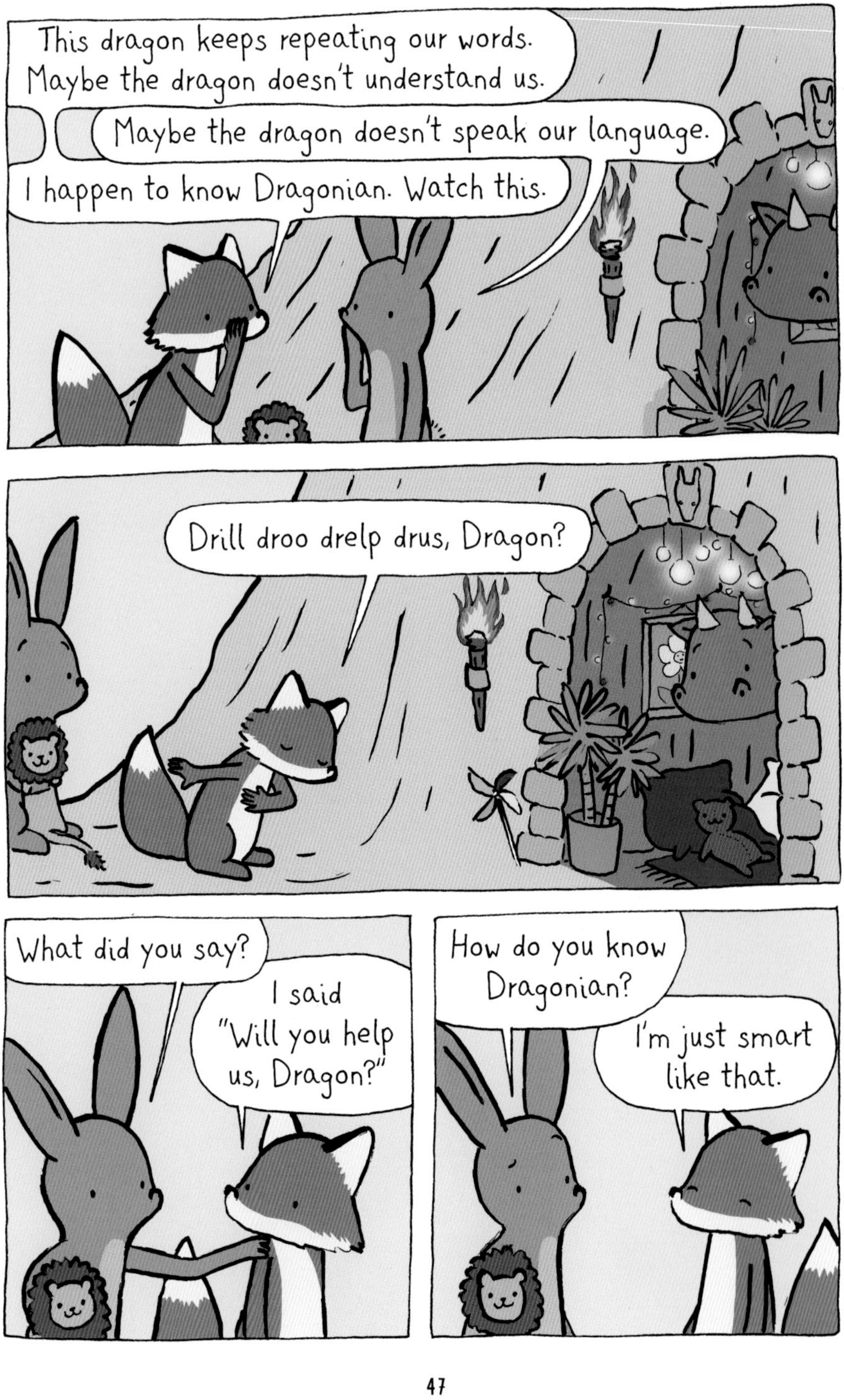
This dragon keeps repeating our words. Maybe the dragon doesn't understand us.
Maybe the dragon doesn't speak our language.
I happen to know Dragonian. Watch this.
Drill droo drelp drus, Dragon?
What did you say?
I said "Will you help us, Dragon?"
How do you know Dragonian?
I'm just smart like that.

Do you think Dragon understands?

I don't know.

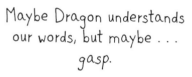

Maybe Dragon understands our words, but maybe . . . gasp.

Maybe Dragon's never had a pizza. Or a birthday.

Or a party?

Or, double gasp, a friend?

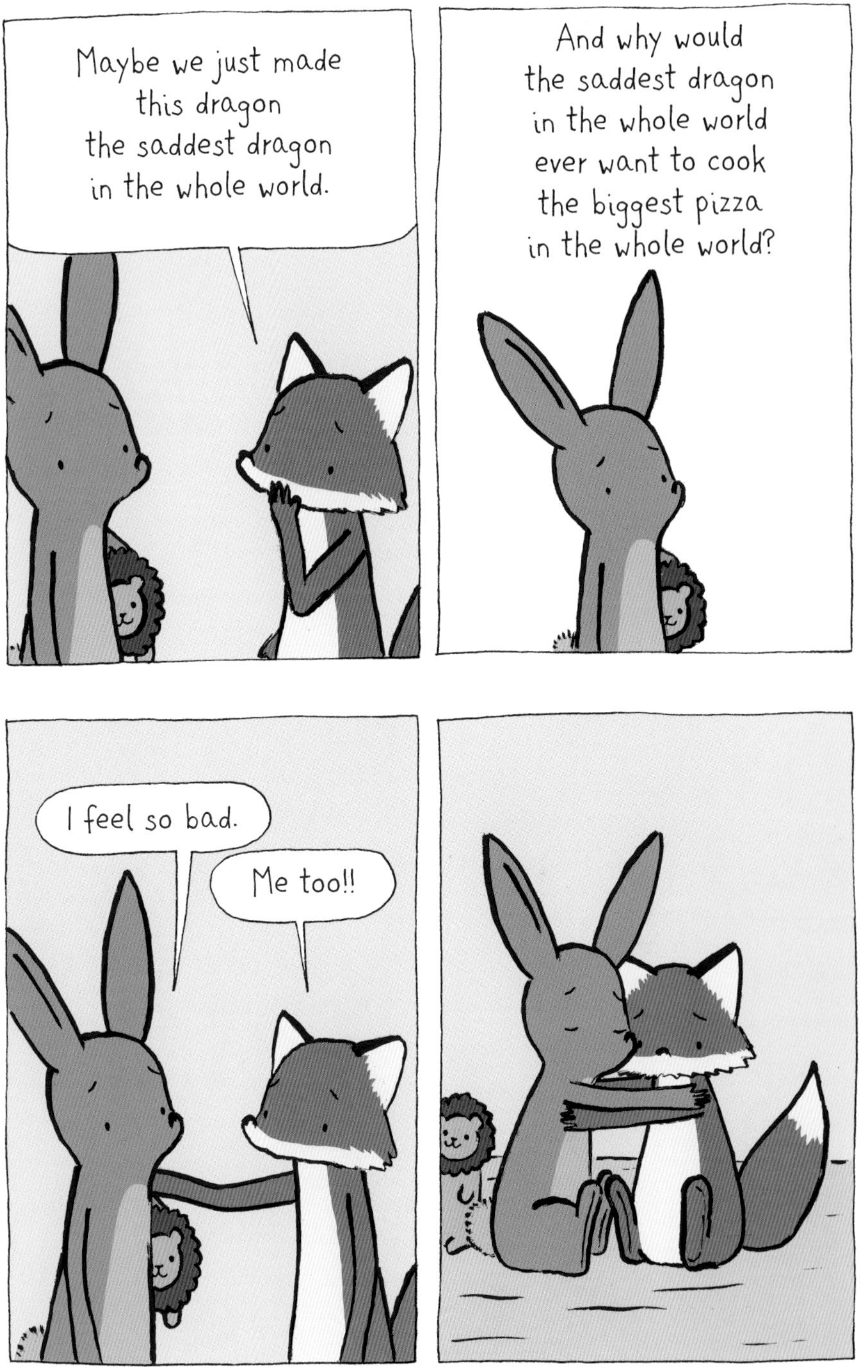
Maybe we just made this dragon the saddest dragon in the whole world.
And why would the saddest dragon in the whole world ever want to cook the biggest pizza in the whole world?
I feel so bad.
Me too!!

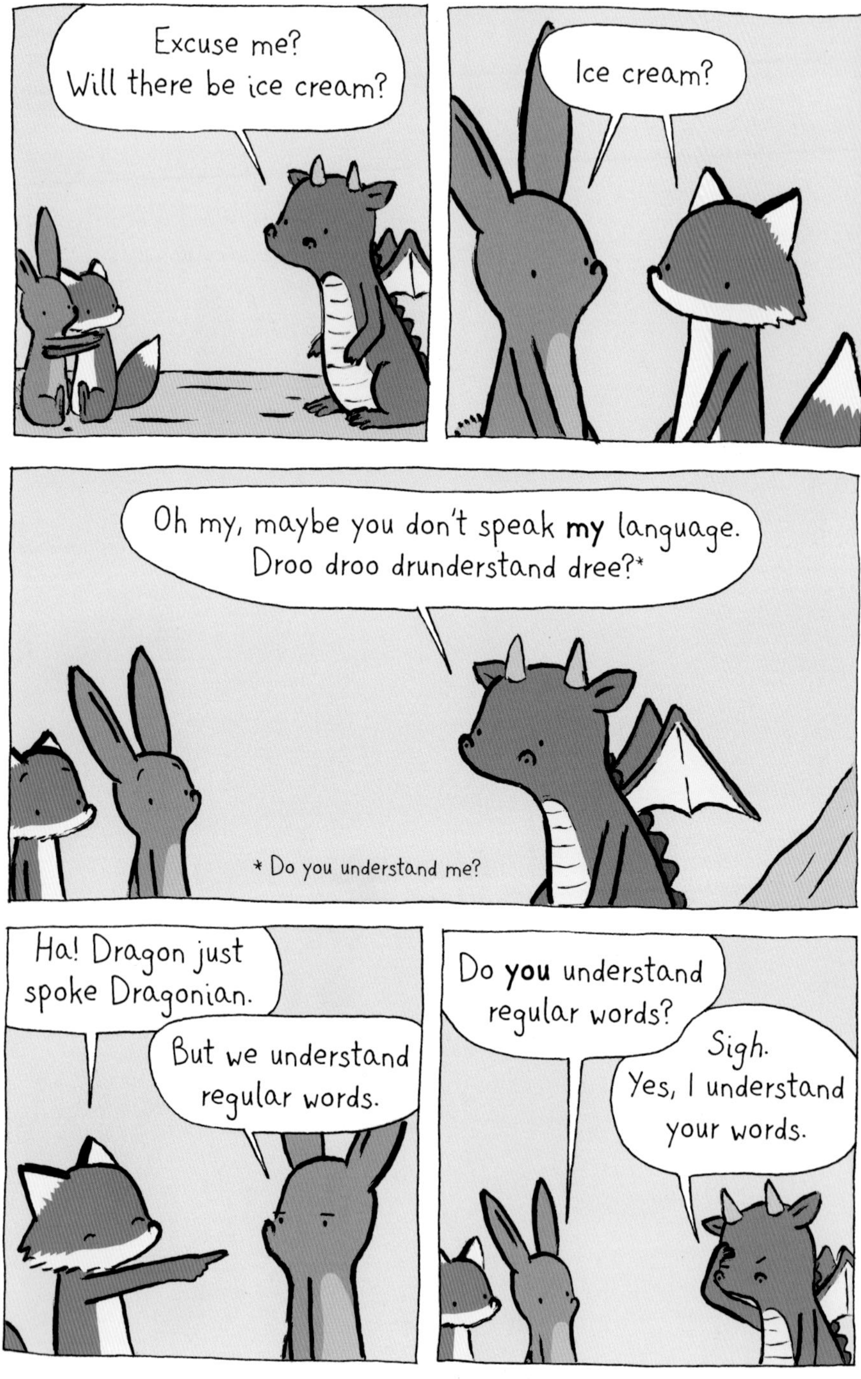
Excuse me?
Will there be ice cream?
Ice cream?
Oh my, maybe you don't speak **my** language.
Droo droo drunderstand dree?*
* Do you understand me?
Ha! Dragon just
spoke Dragonian.
But we understand
regular words.
Do **you** understand
regular words?
Sigh.
Yes, I understand
your words.

It's everything else I don't understand. Why haven't I ever been invited to a party? Why is the sky blue? What does ice cream taste like? What does having a friend feel like?

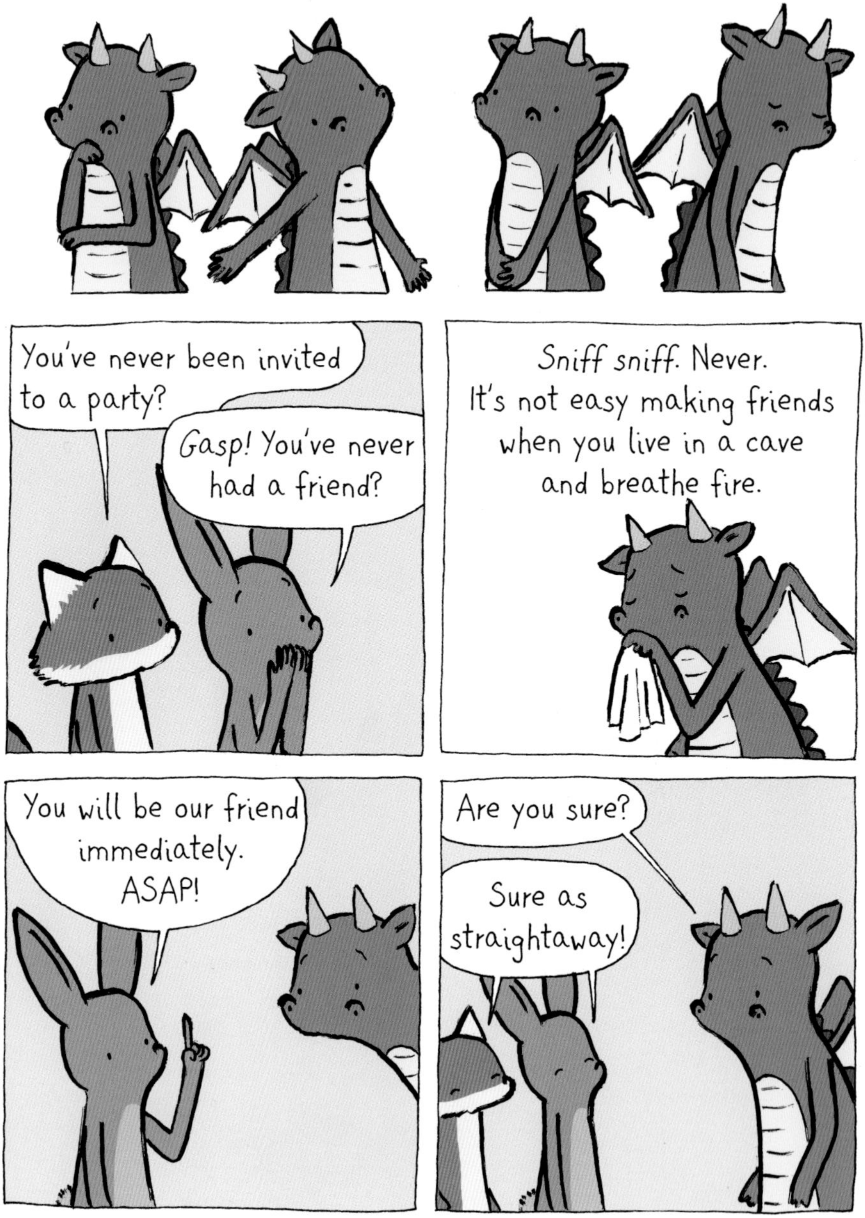
You've never been invited to a party?
Gasp! You've never had a friend?
Sniff sniff. Never. It's not easy making friends when you live in a cave and breathe fire.
You will be our friend immediately. ASAP!
Are you sure?
Sure as straightaway!

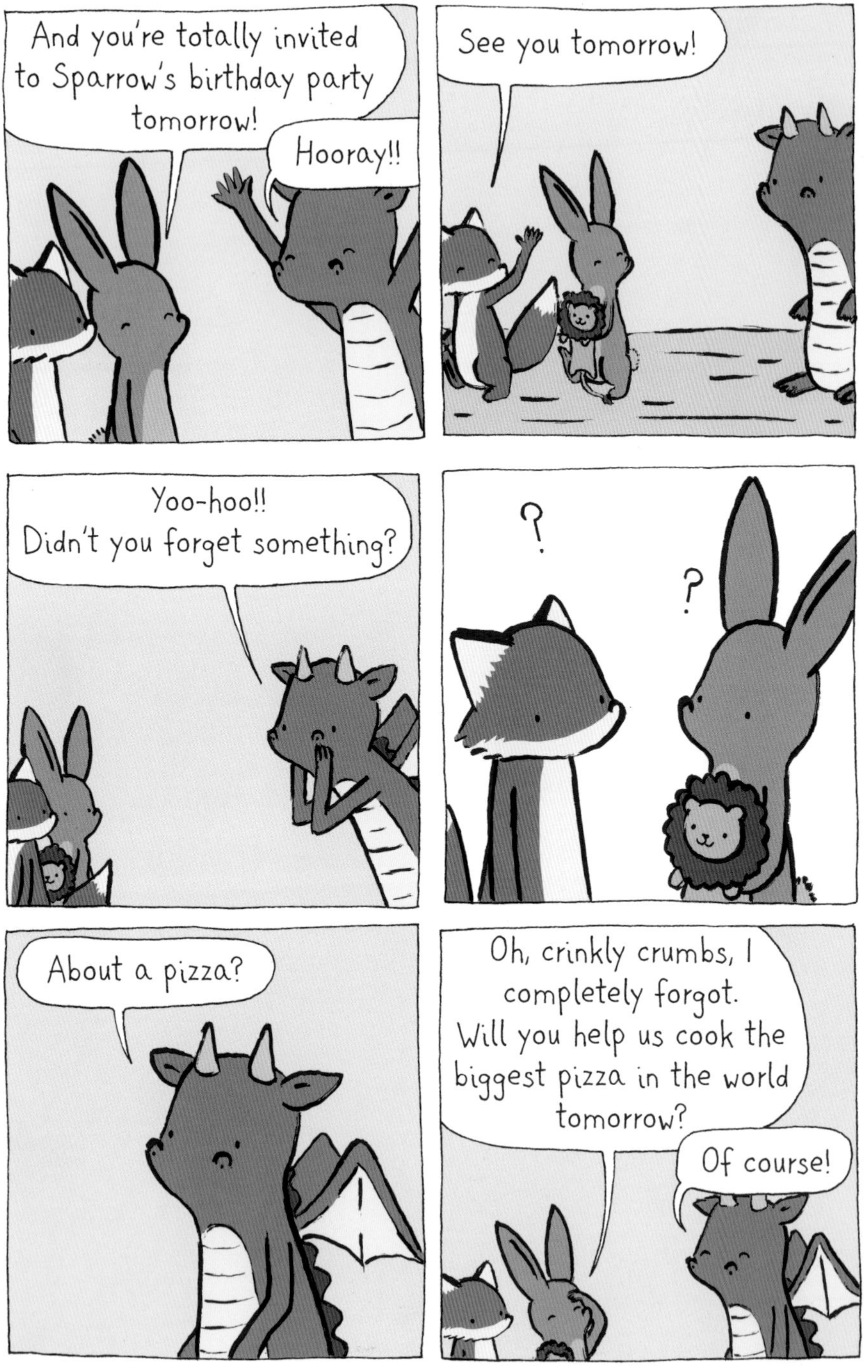
And you're totally invited to Sparrow's birthday party tomorrow!
Hooray!!
See you tomorrow!
Yoo-hoo!! Didn't you forget something?
?
?
About a pizza?
Oh, crinkly crumbs, I completely forgot. Will you help us cook the biggest pizza in the world tomorrow?
Of course!

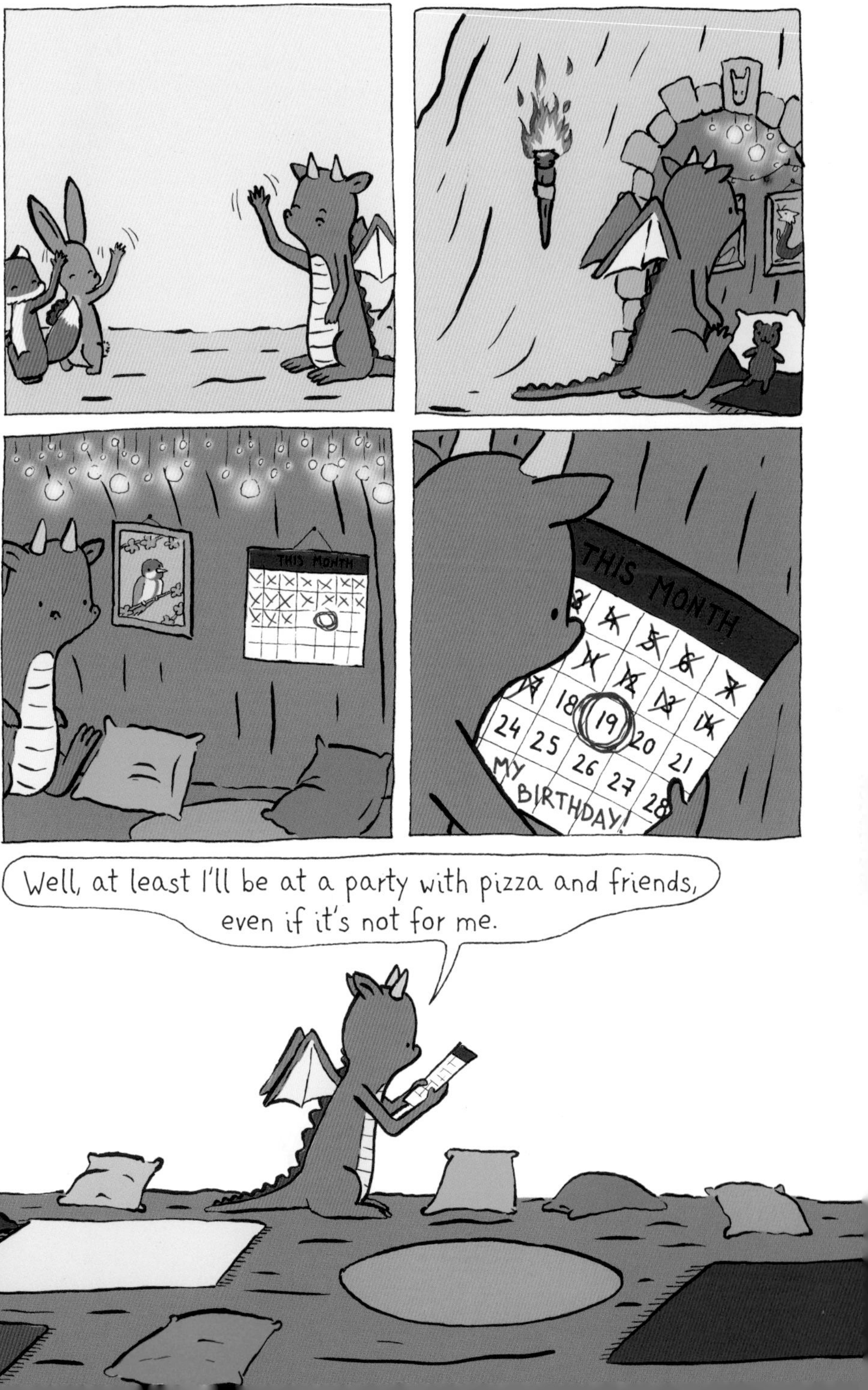
THIS MONTH
THIS MONTH
18 19 20 21
24 25 26 27 28
MY BIRTHDAY!
Well, at least I'll be at a party with pizza and friends, even if it's not for me.

BIRTHDAYS,
BEST DAYS
& BEST FRIENDS

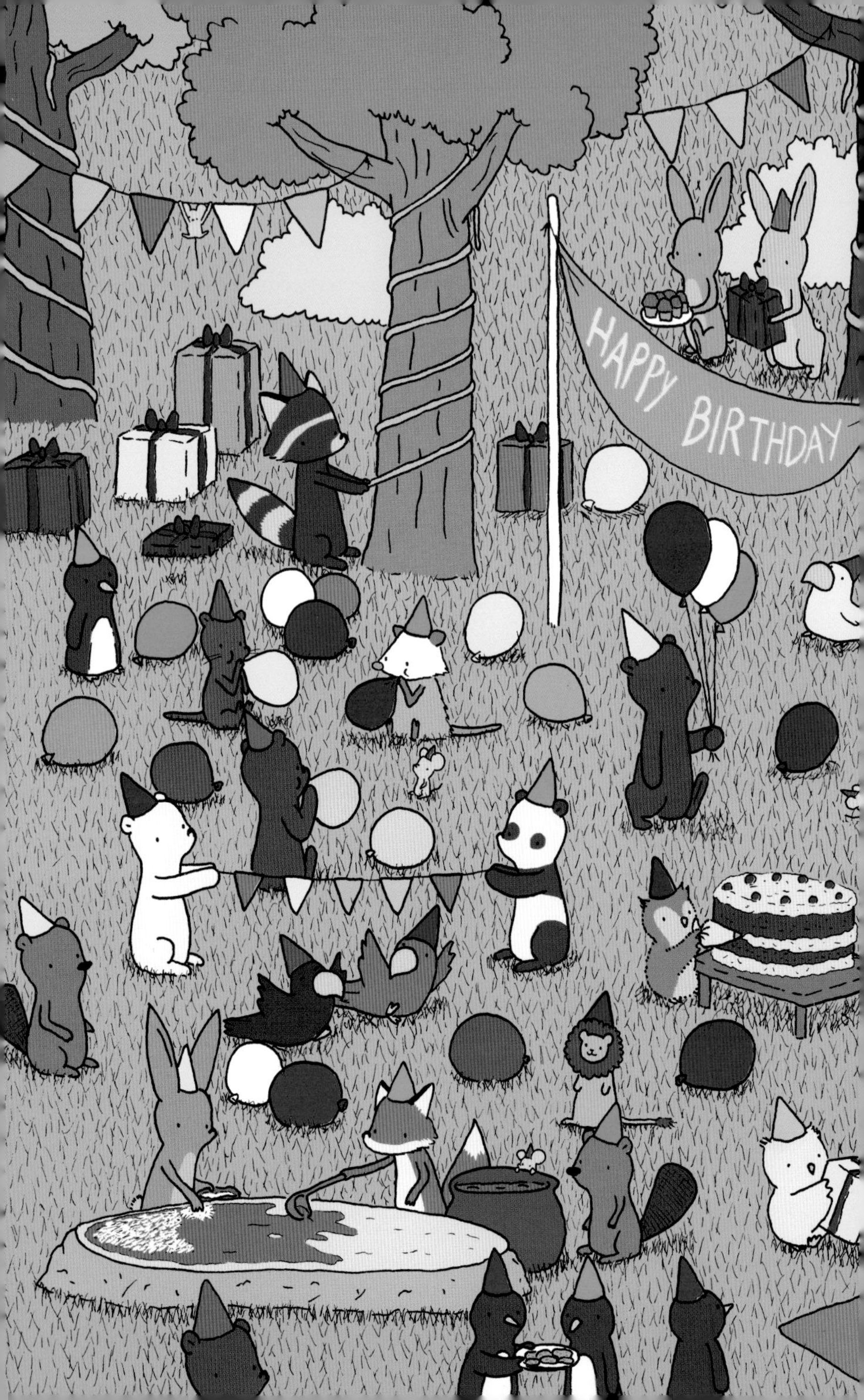
HAPPY BIRTHDAY

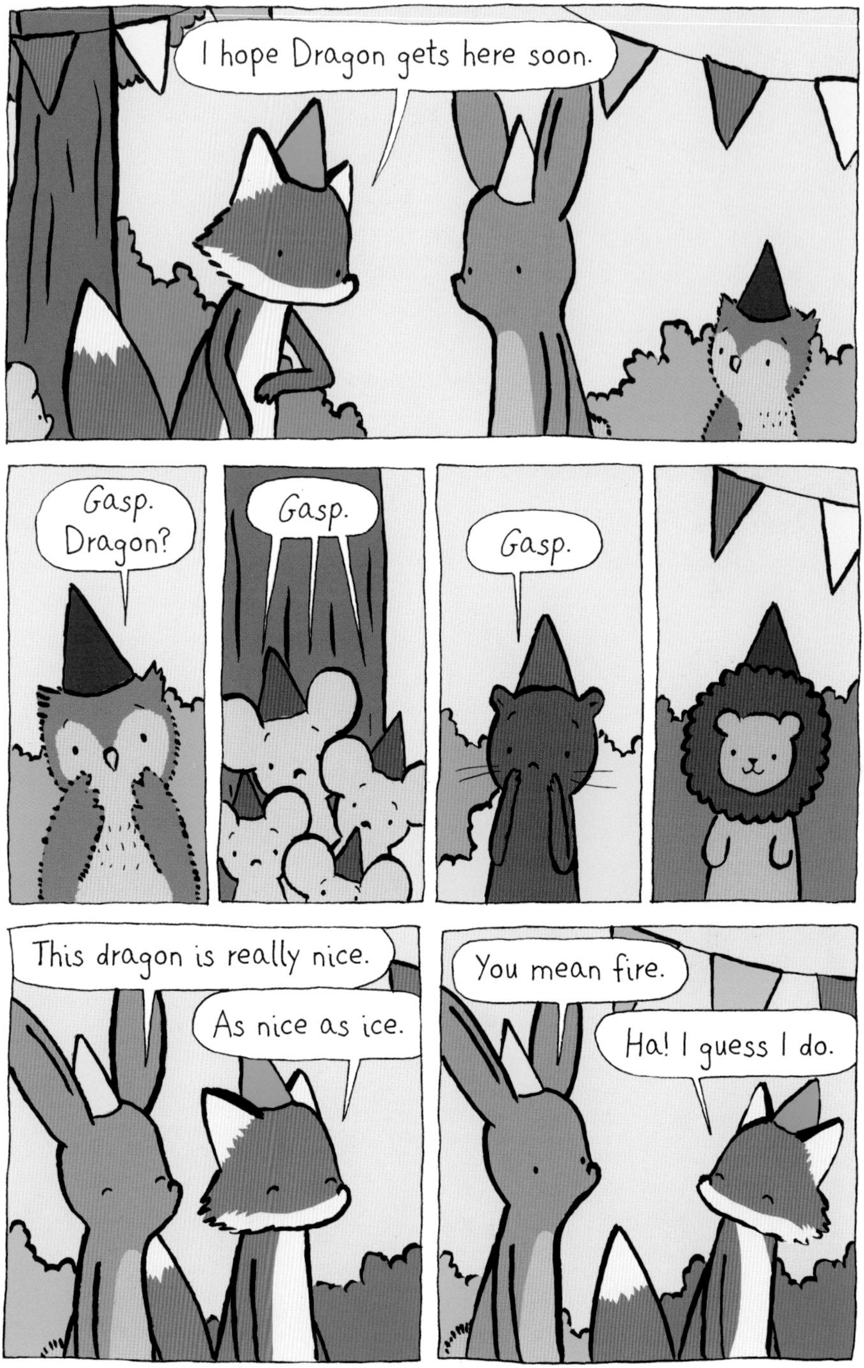
I hope Dragon gets here soon.
Gasp.
Dragon?
Gasp.
Gasp.
This dragon is really nice.
As nice as ice.
You mean fire.
Ha! I guess I do.

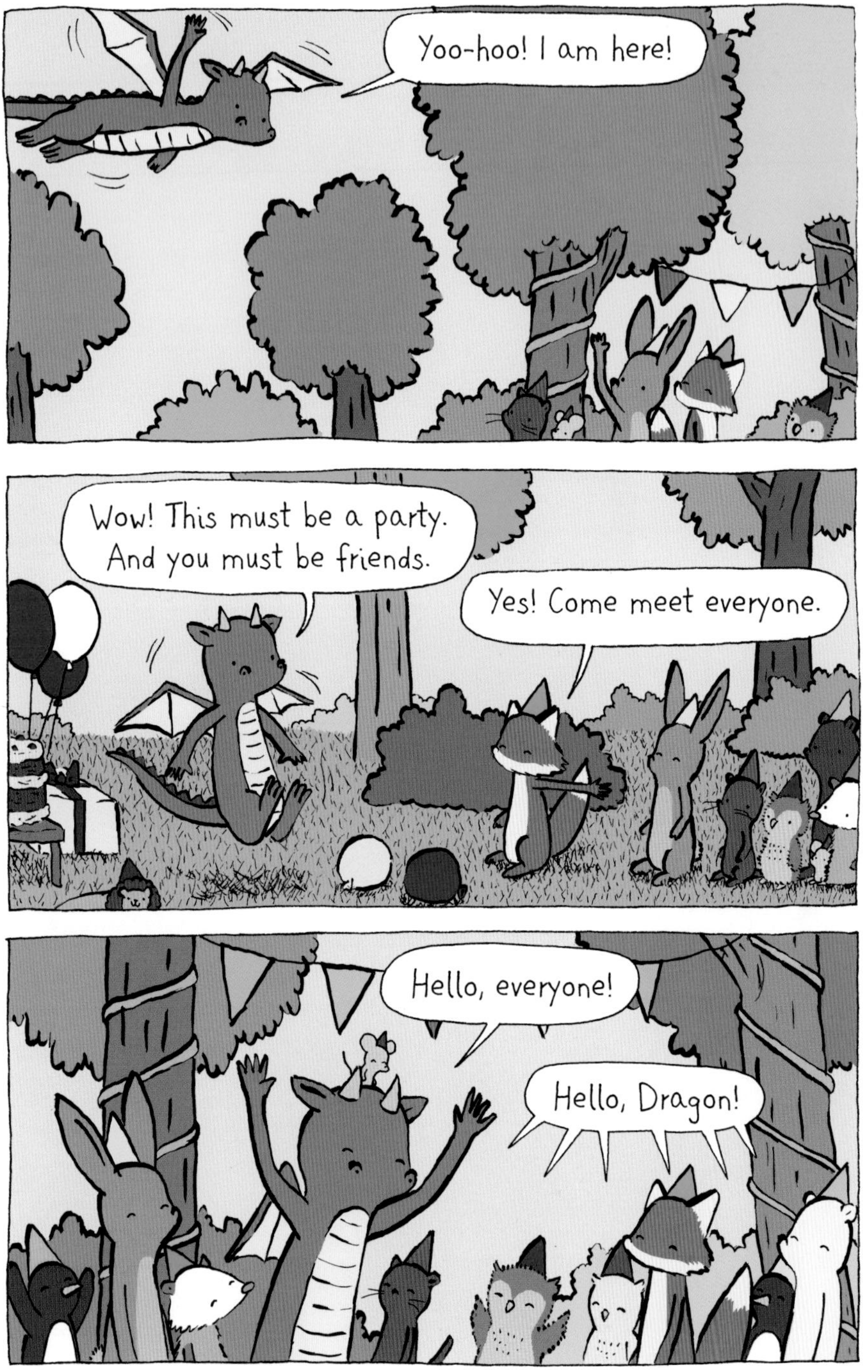
Yoo-hoo! I am here!
Wow! This must be a party. And you must be friends.
Yes! Come meet everyone.
Hello, everyone!
Hello, Dragon!

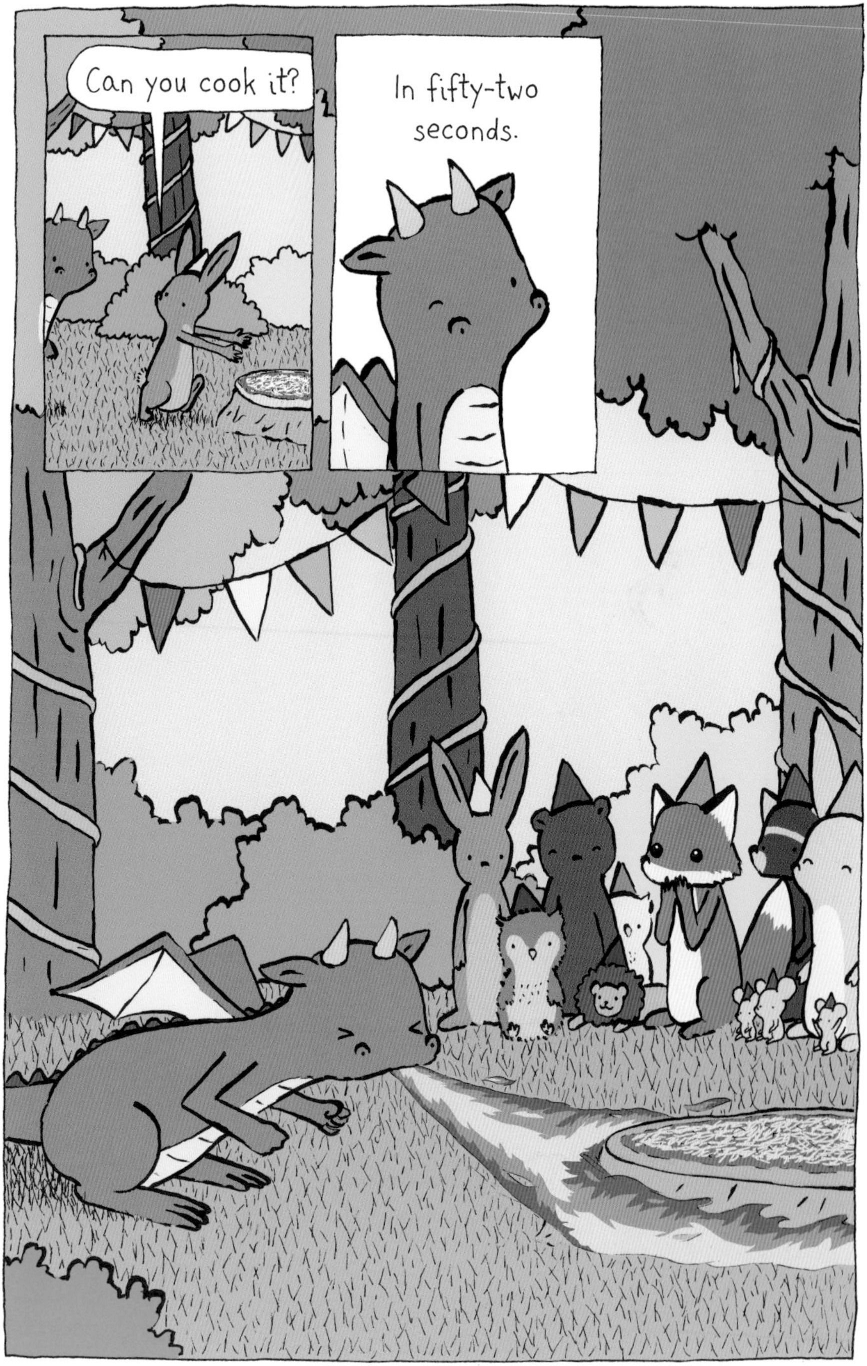
Can you cook it?
In fifty-two seconds.

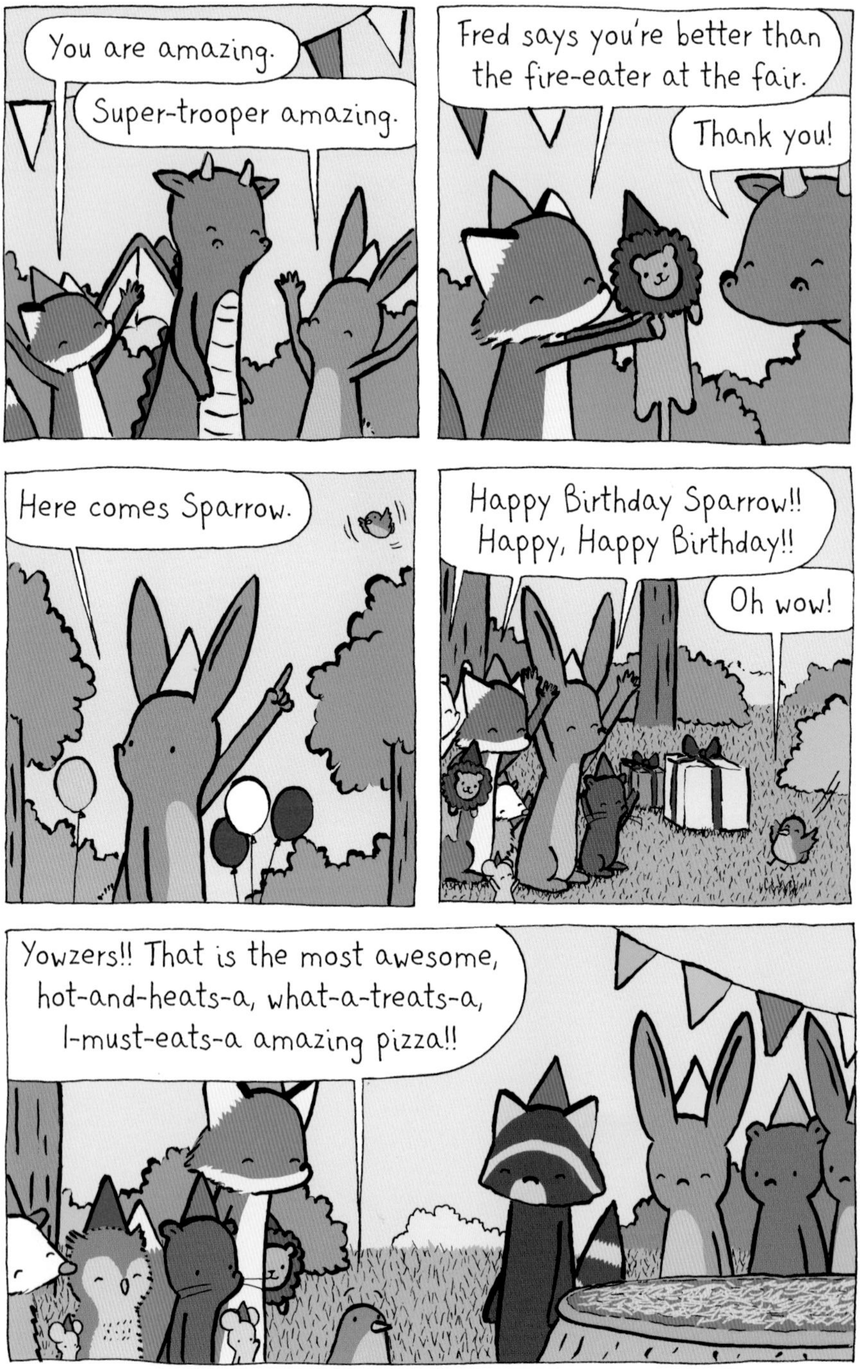
You are amazing.
Super-trooper amazing.
Fred says you're better than the fire-eater at the fair.
Thank you!
Here comes Sparrow.
Happy Birthday Sparrow!! Happy, Happy Birthday!!
Oh wow!
Yowzers!! That is the most awesome, hot-and-heats-a, what-a-treats-a, I-must-eats-a amazing pizza!!

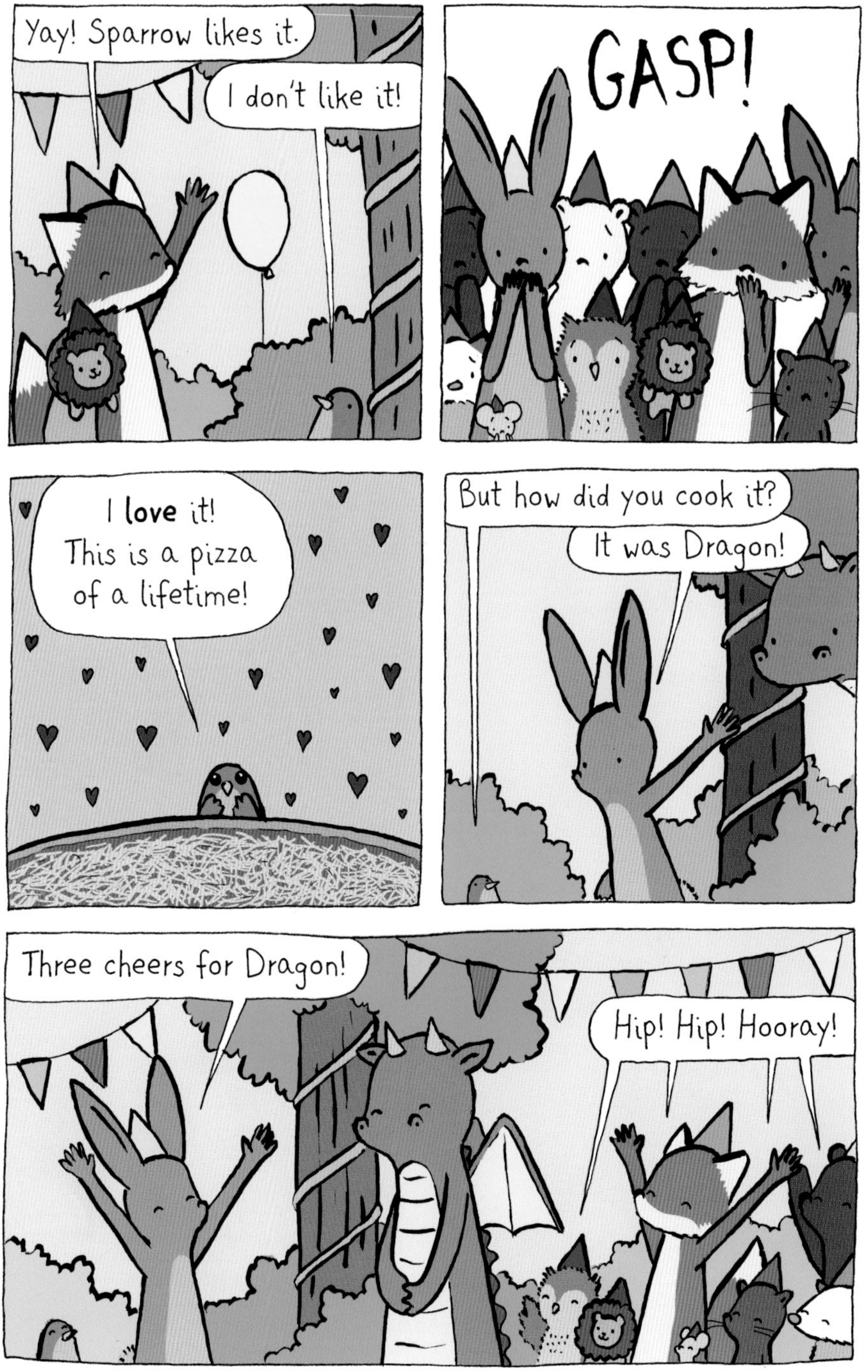
Yay! Sparrow likes it.
I don't like it!
GASP!
I love it!
This is a pizza of a lifetime!
But how did you cook it?
It was Dragon!
Three cheers for Dragon!
Hip! Hip! Hooray!

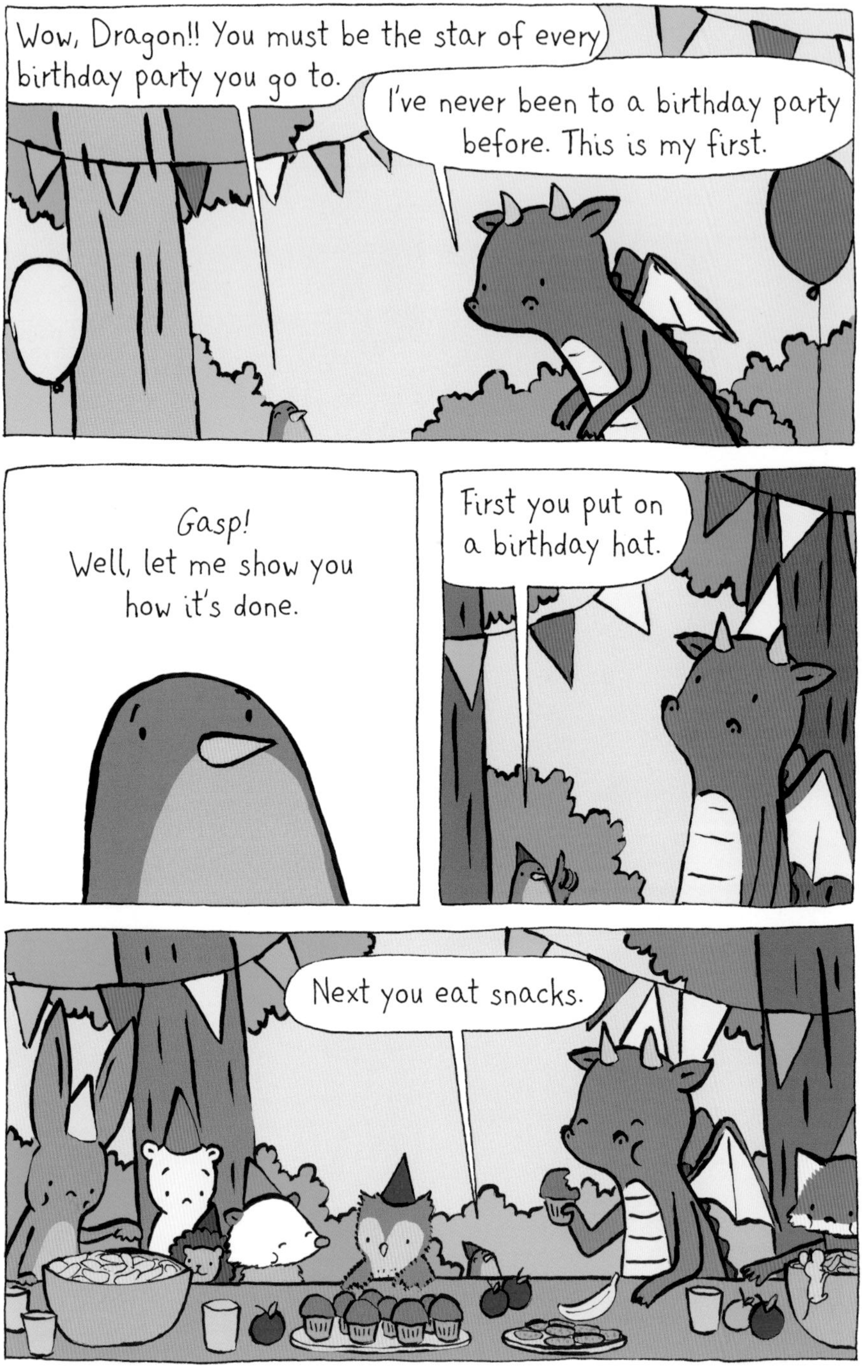
Wow, Dragon!! You must be the star of every birthday party you go to.
I've never been to a birthday party before. This is my first.
Gasp!
Well, let me show you how it's done.
First you put on a birthday hat.
Next you eat snacks.

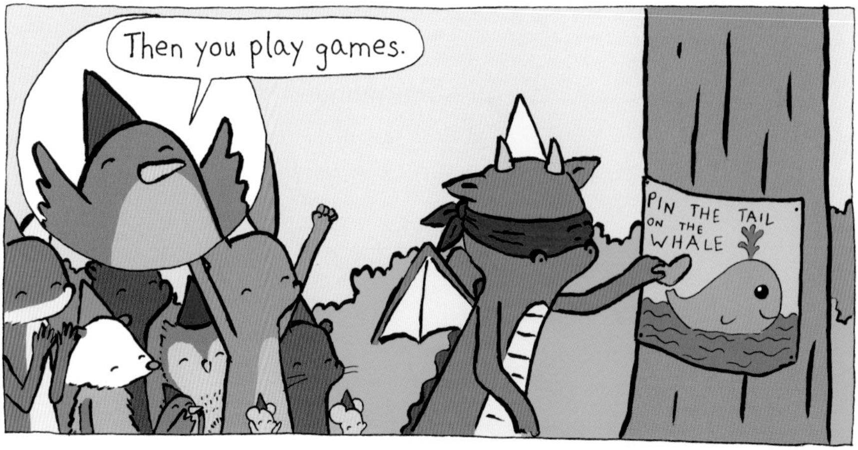
Then you play games.
PIN THE TAIL ON THE WHALE

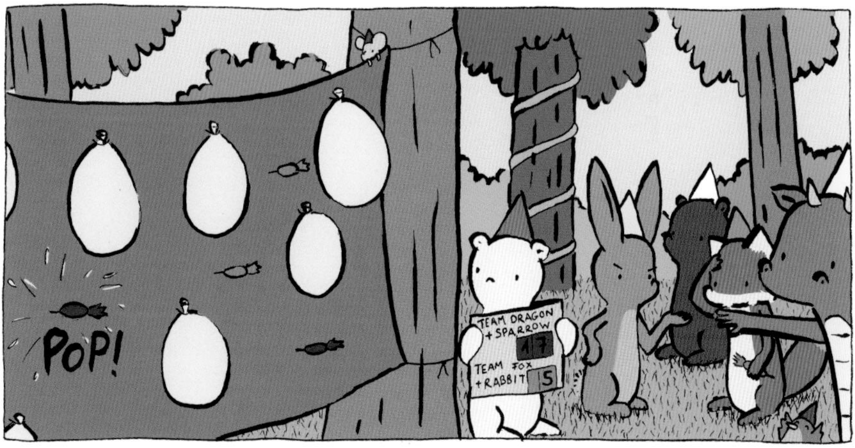
POP!
TEAM DRAGON + SPARROW 17
TEAM FOX + RABBIT 15

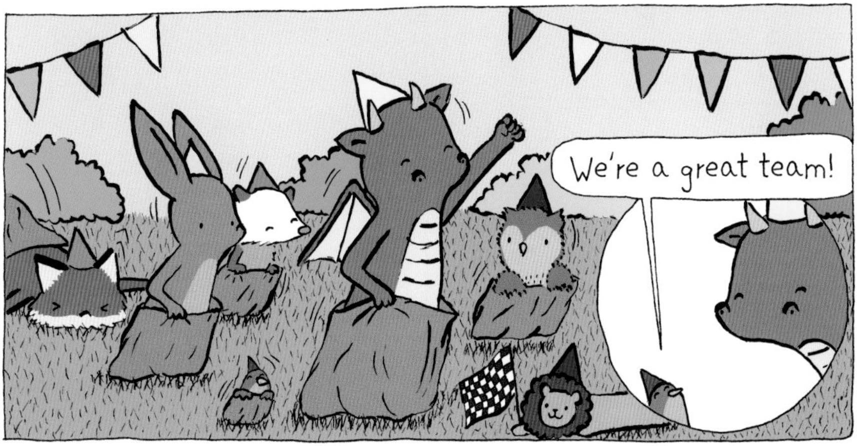
We're a great team!

Then it's time for pizza!
The biggest, bestest, greatest, home-madest pizza in the whole world.

This is the best pizza I've ever had.
In fact, it's the only pizza I've ever had.

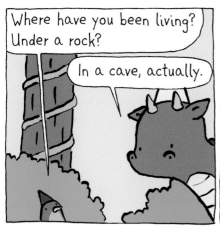

Where have you been living? Under a rock?

In a cave, actually.

And after you're completely exhausted and stuffed, then it's time for cake! Birthdays are great, but birthday food is the greatest!

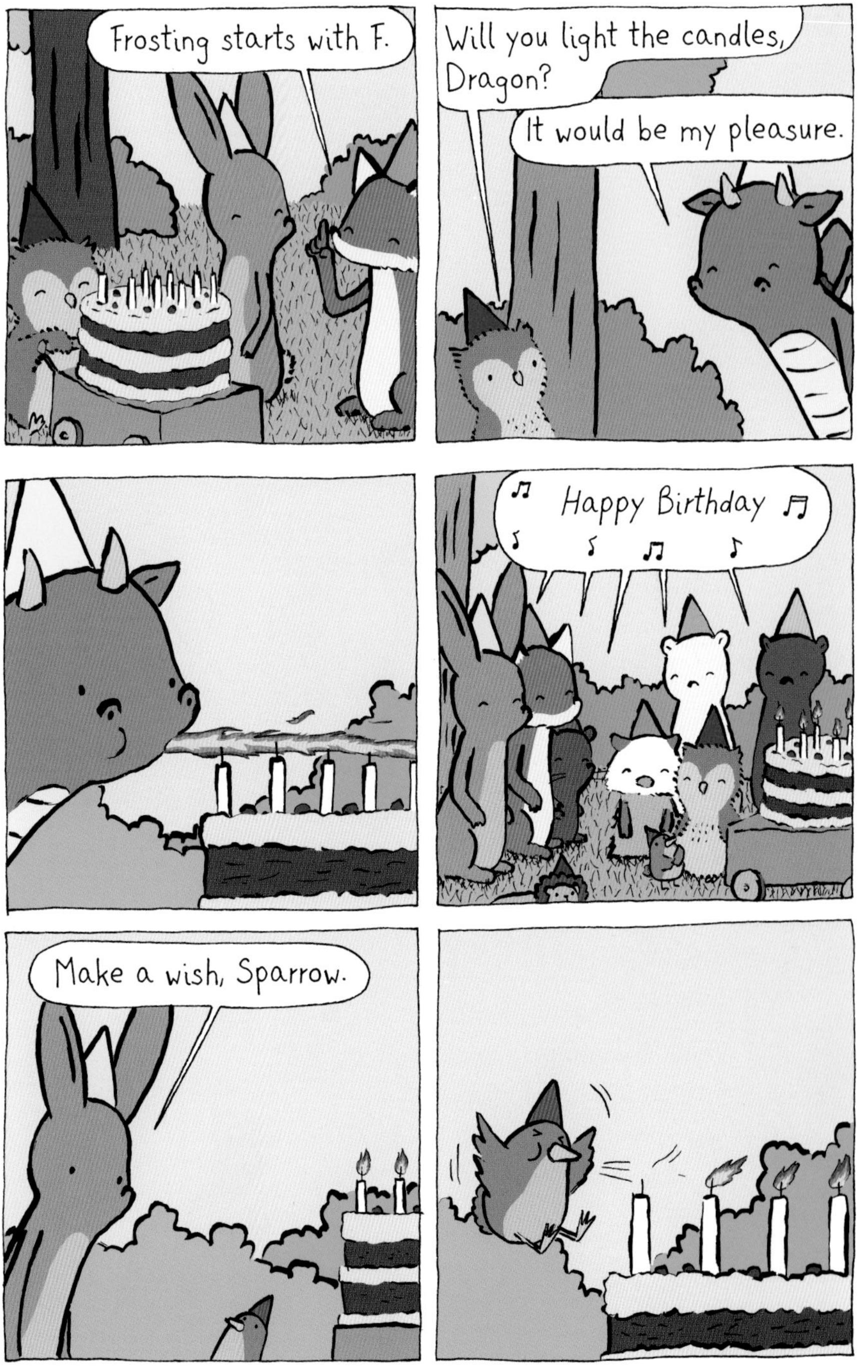
Frosting starts with F.
Will you light the candles, Dragon?
It would be my pleasure.
Happy Birthday
Make a wish, Sparrow.

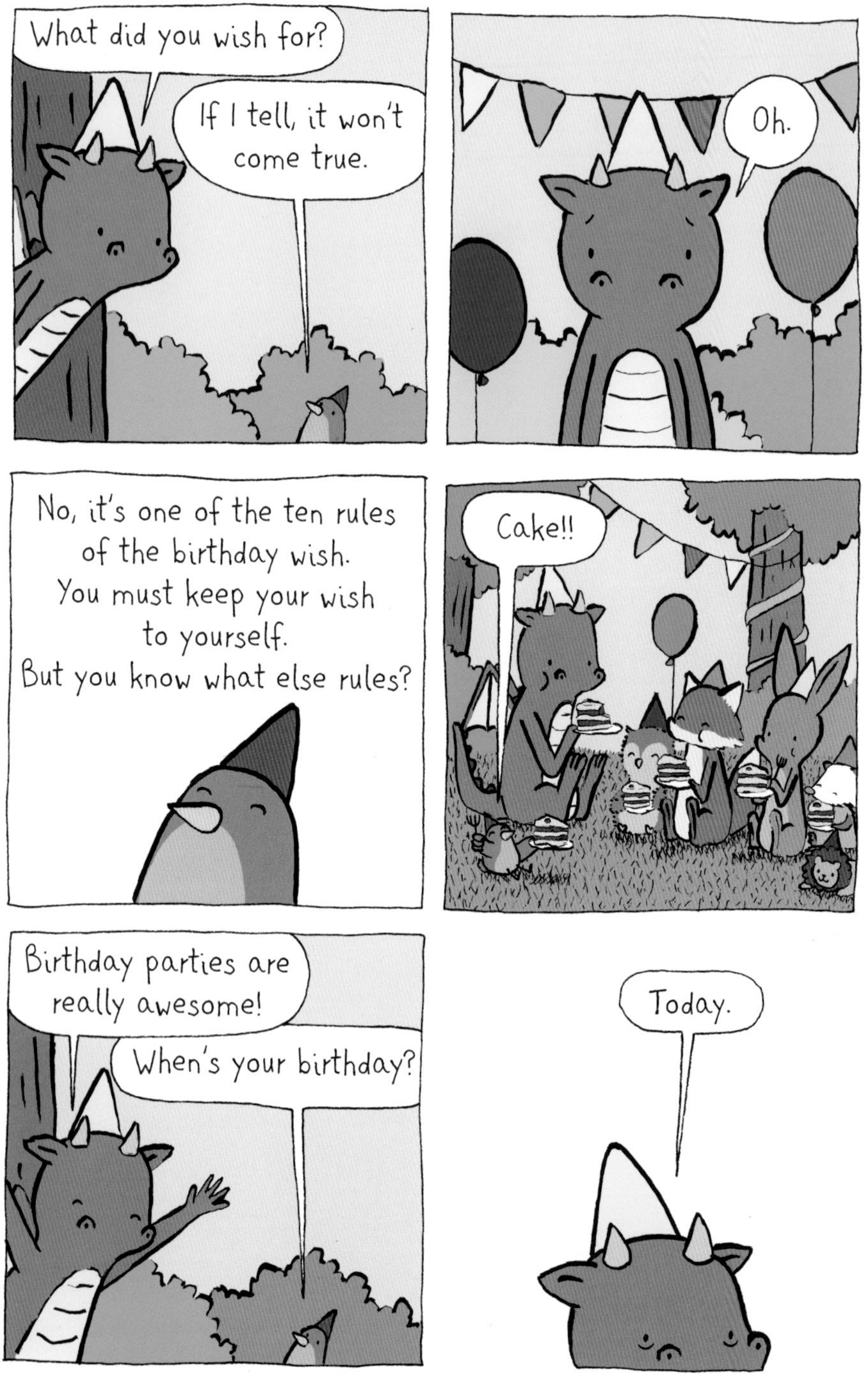
What did you wish for?
If I tell, it won't come true.
Oh.
No, it's one of the ten rules of the birthday wish. You must keep your wish to yourself. But you know what else rules?
Cake!!
Birthday parties are really awesome!
When's your birthday?
Today.

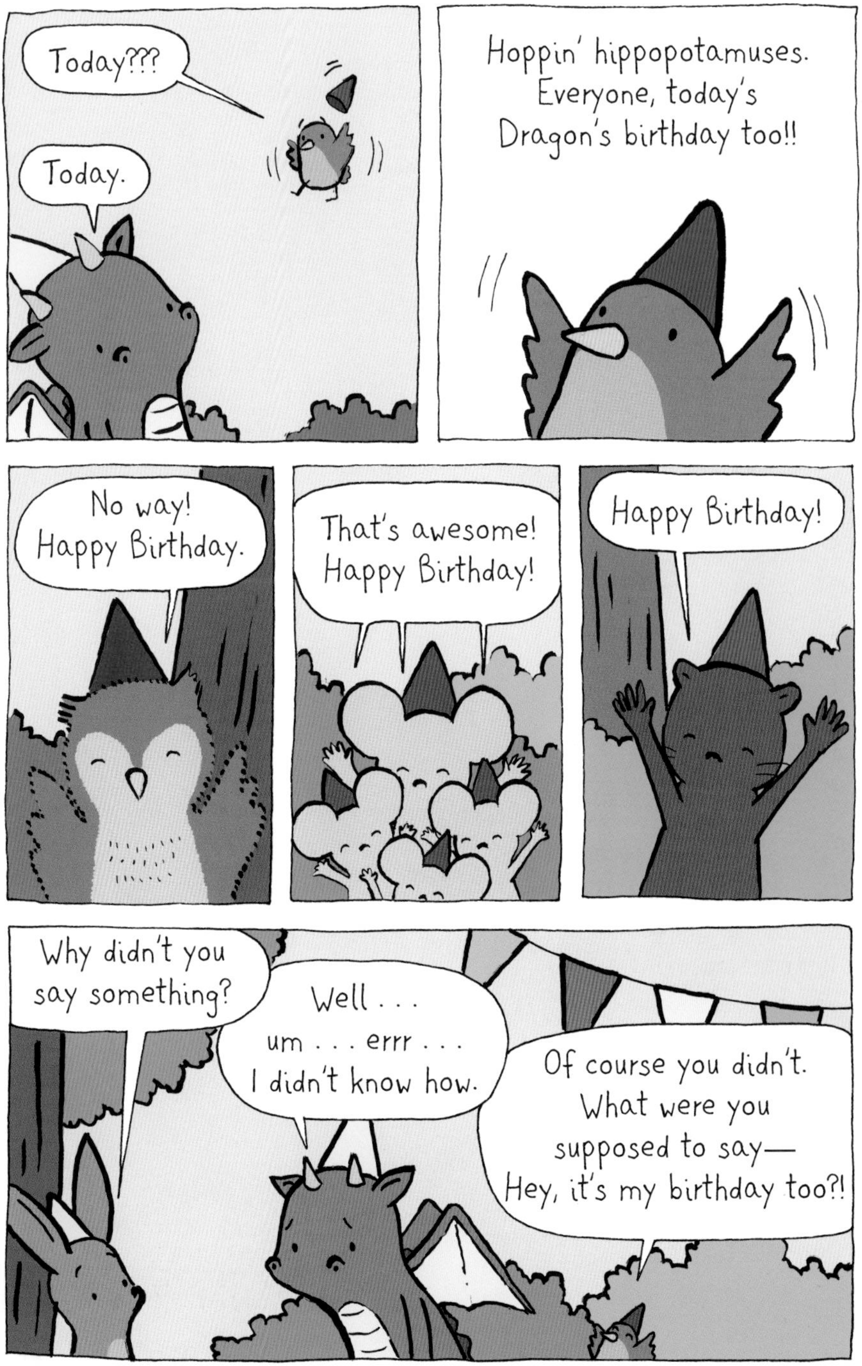
Today???
Today.
Hoppin' hippopotamuses. Everyone, today's Dragon's birthday too!!
No way! Happy Birthday.
That's awesome! Happy Birthday!
Happy Birthday!
Why didn't you say something?
Well . . . um . . . errr . . . I didn't know how.
Of course you didn't. What were you supposed to say— Hey, it's my birthday too?!

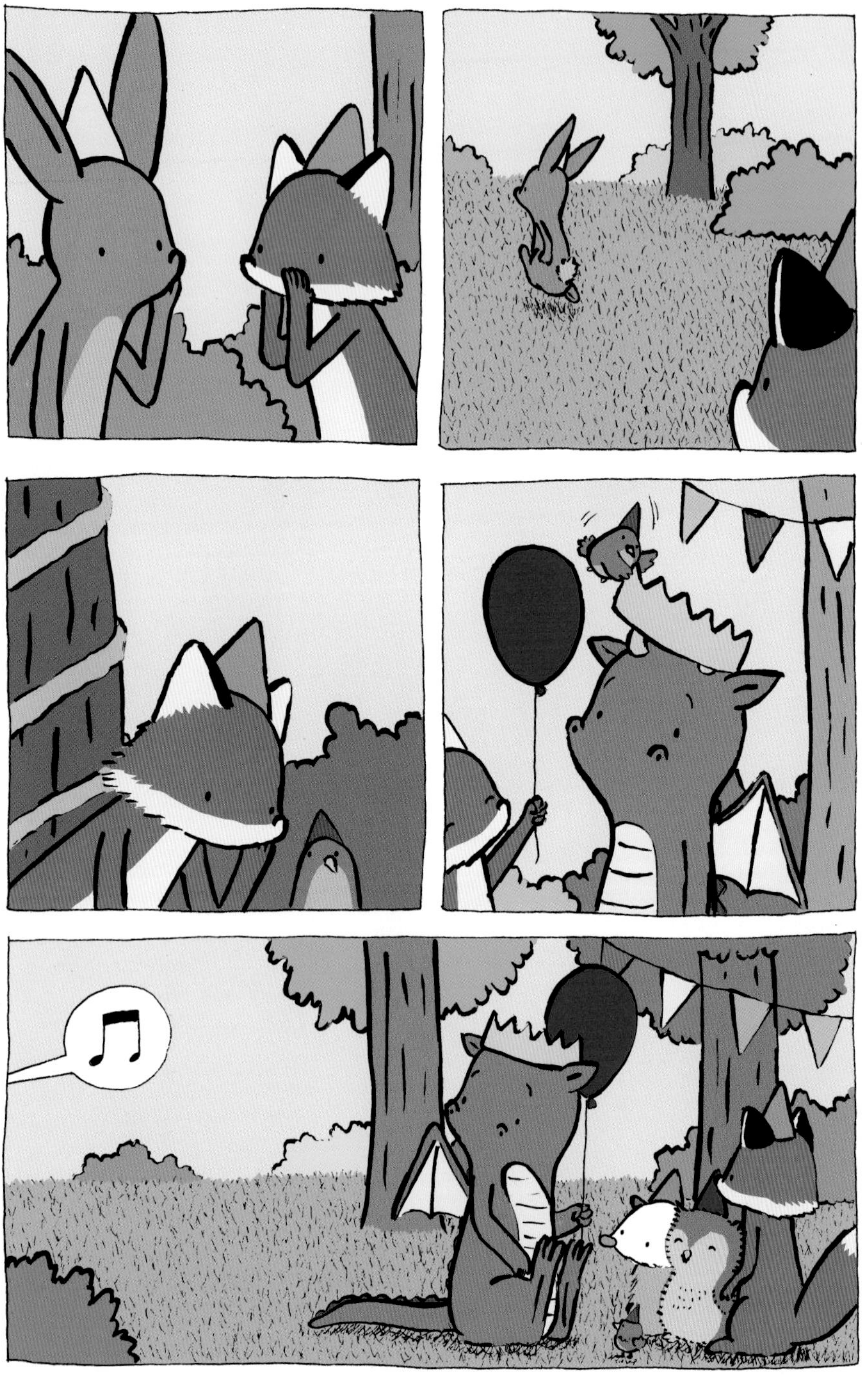

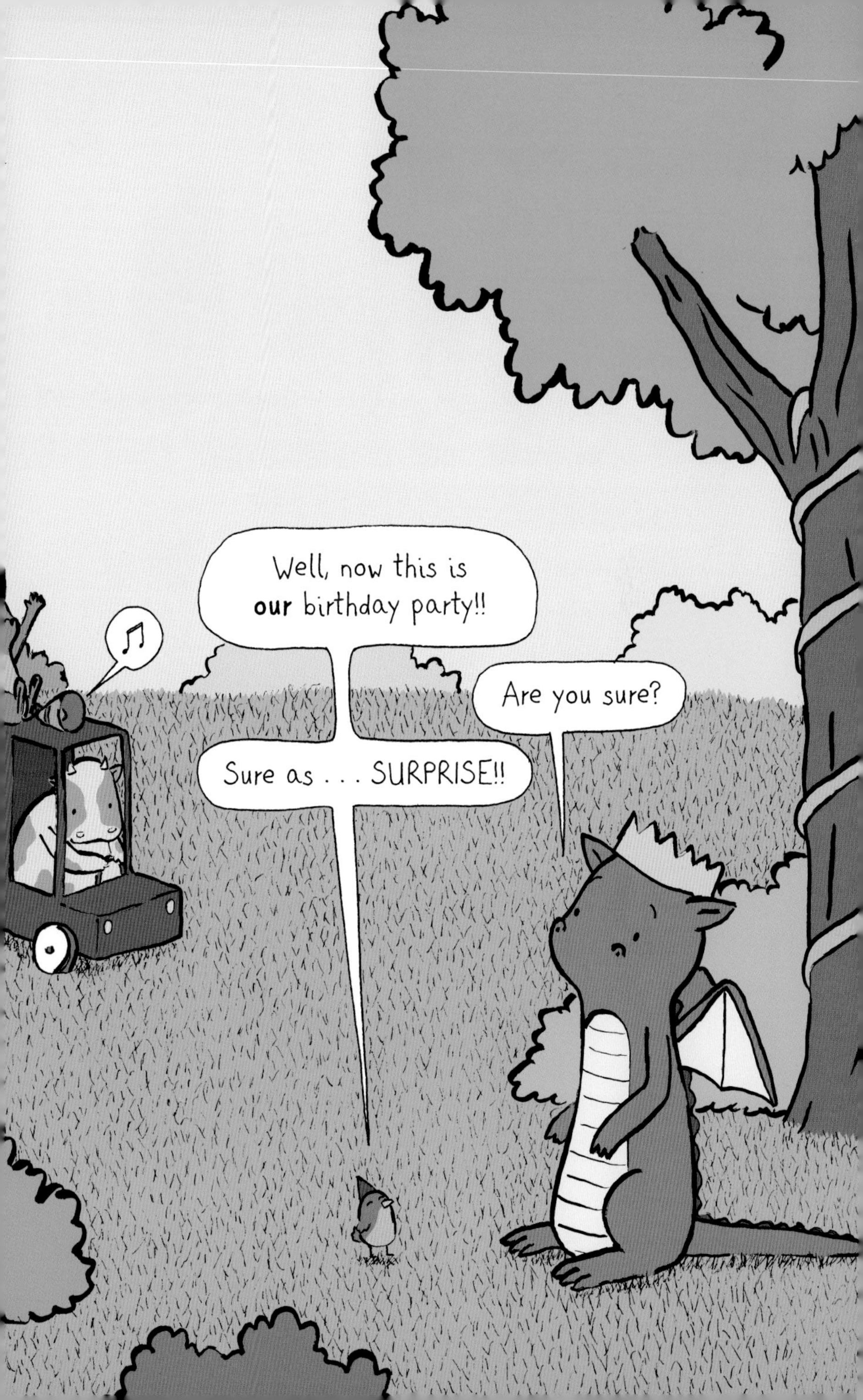
♫
Well, now this is **our** birthday party!!
Are you sure?
Sure as . . . SURPRISE!!

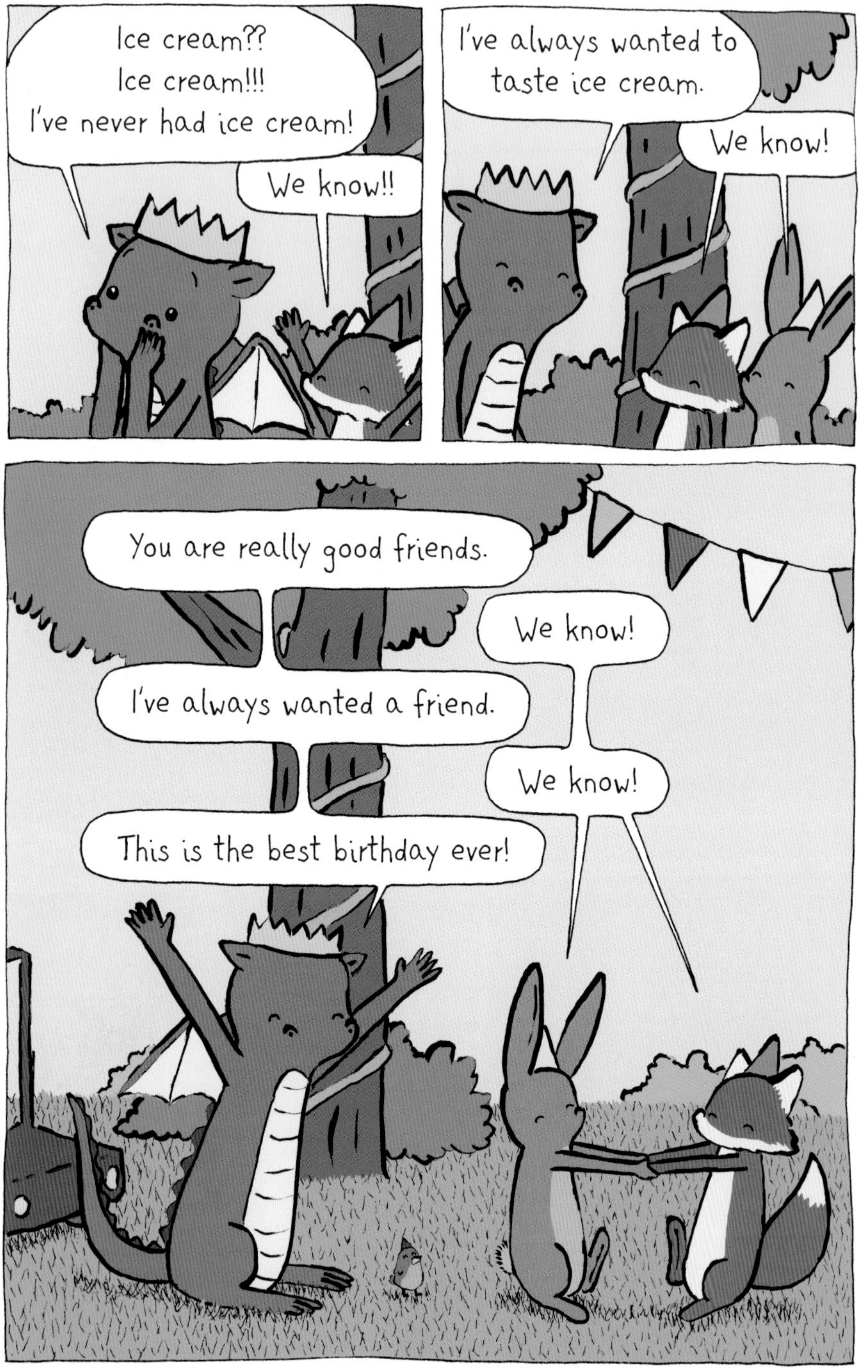
Ice cream??
Ice cream!!!
I've never had ice cream!
We know!!
I've always wanted to taste ice cream.
We know!
You are really good friends.
We know!
I've always wanted a friend.
We know!
This is the best birthday ever!

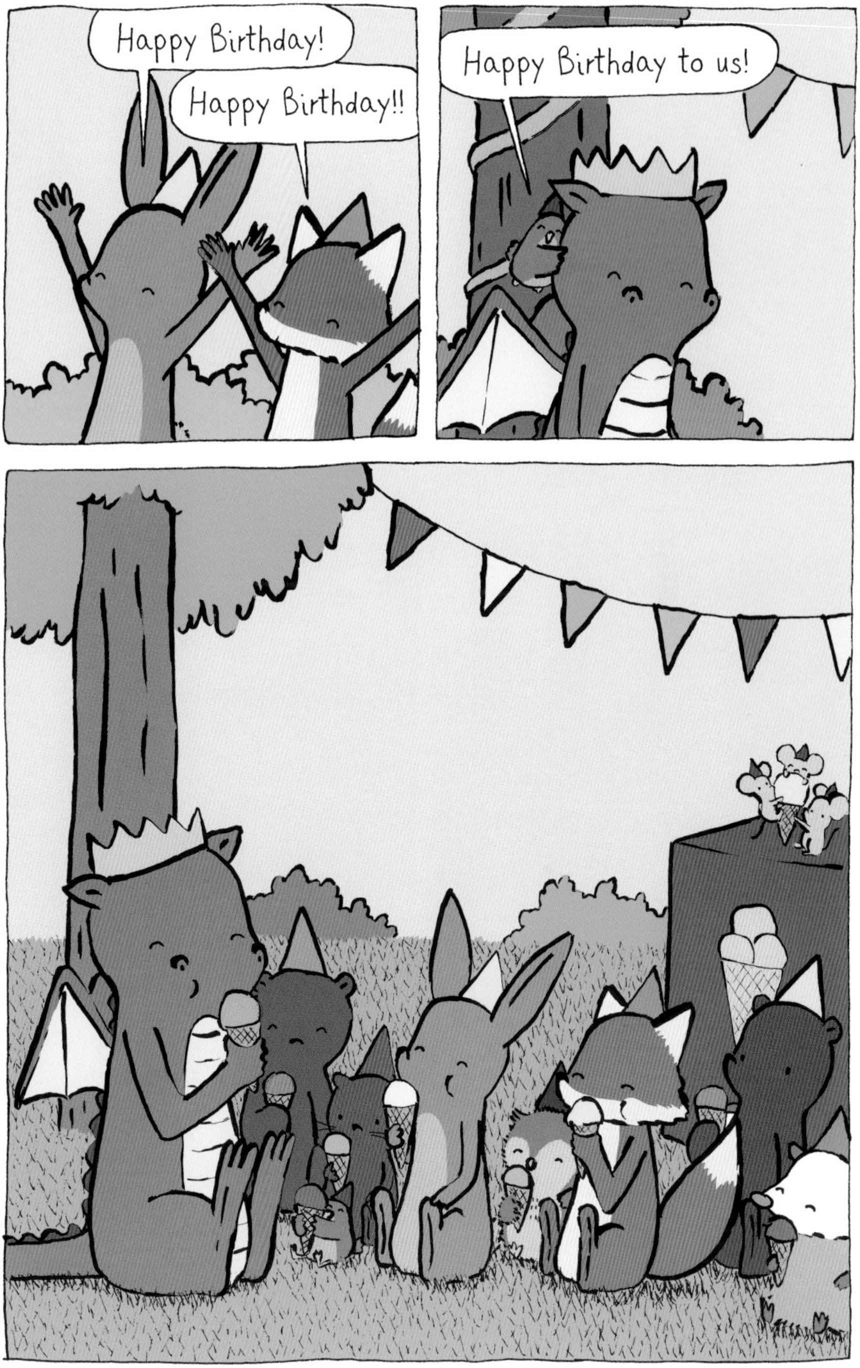
Happy Birthday!
Happy Birthday!!
Happy Birthday to us!

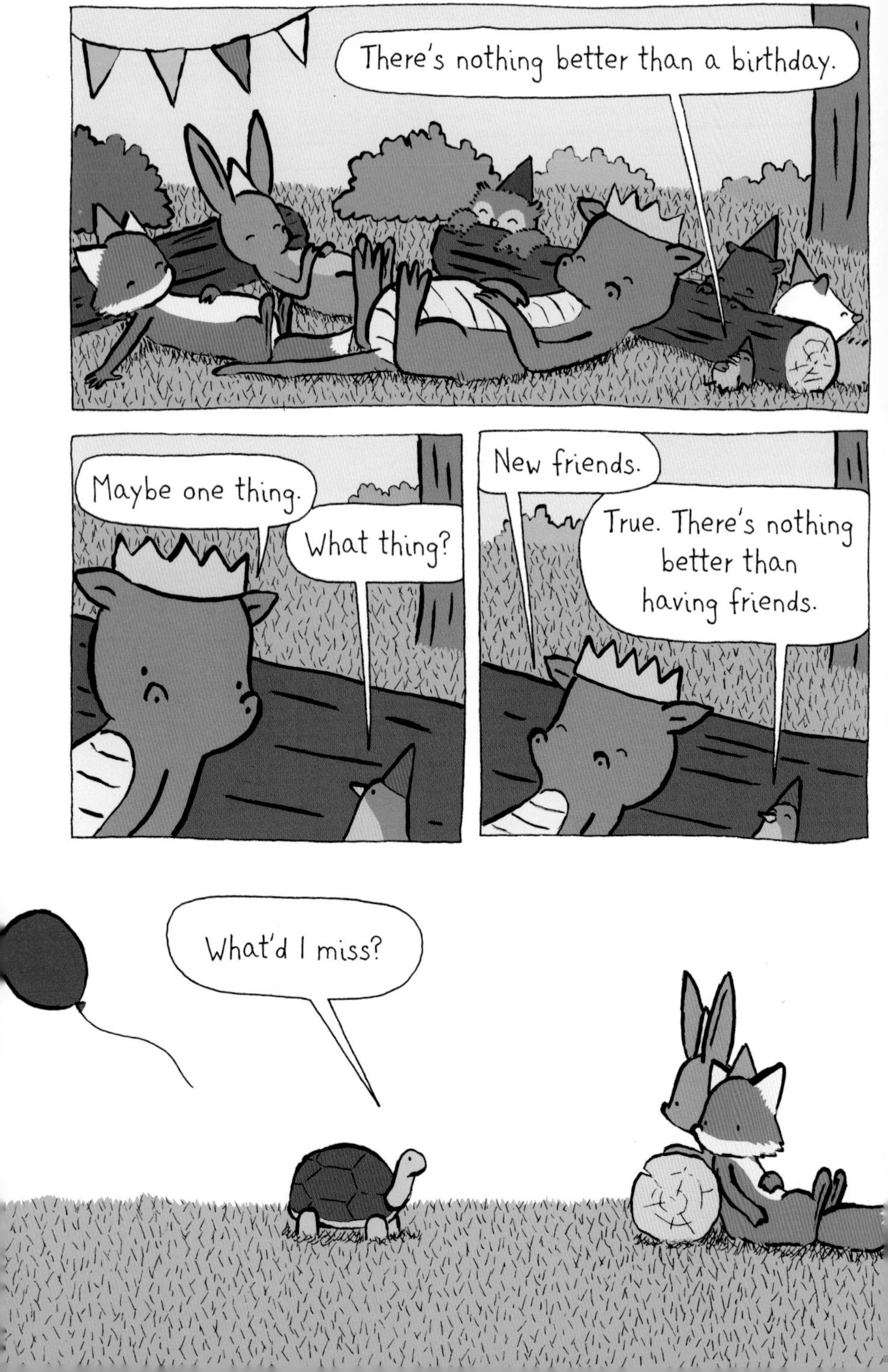
There's nothing better than a birthday.
Maybe one thing.
What thing?
New friends.
True. There's nothing better than having friends.
What'd I miss?

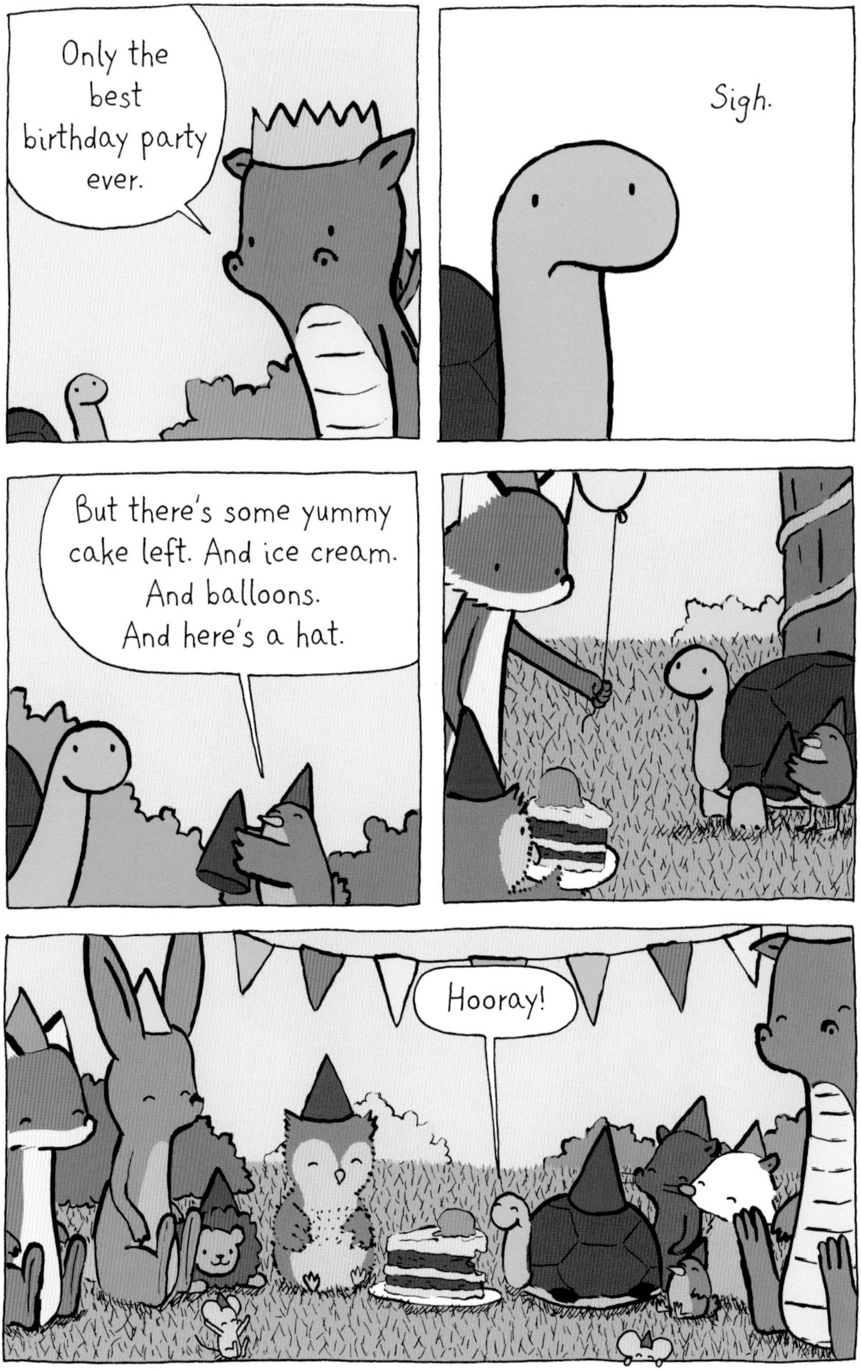
Only the best birthday party ever.
Sigh.
But there's some yummy cake left. And ice cream. And balloons. And here's a hat.
Hooray!

STORY FIVE

WONDER, WISH & WOW

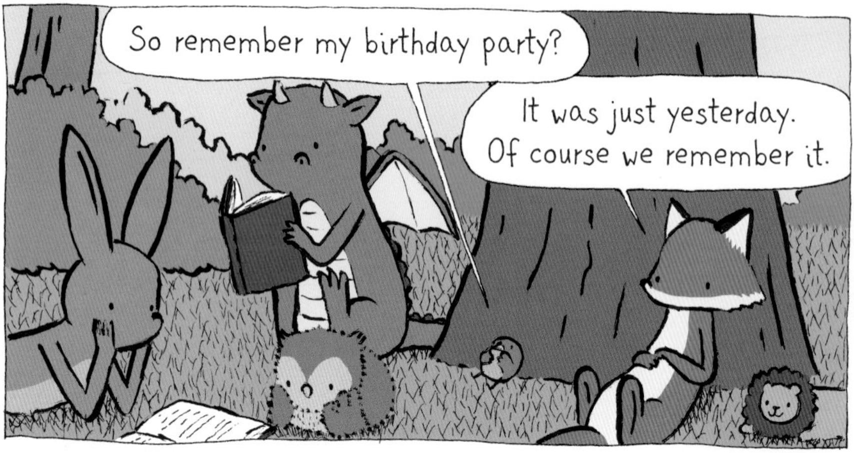
So remember my birthday party?
It was just yesterday. Of course we remember it.

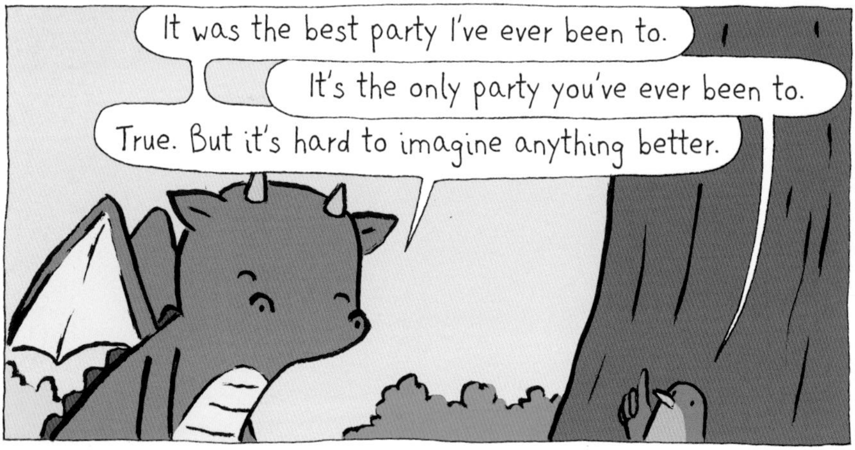
It was the best party I've ever been to.
It's the only party you've ever been to.
True. But it's hard to imagine anything better.

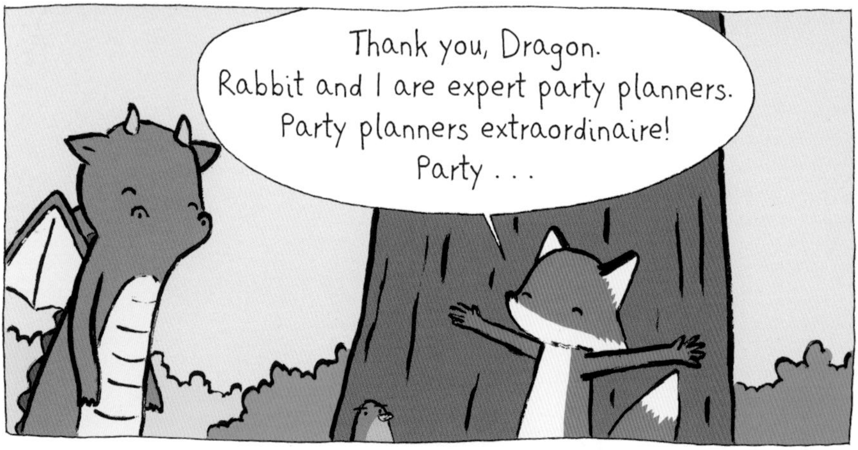
Thank you, Dragon. Rabbit and I are expert party planners. Party planners extraordinaire! Party . . .

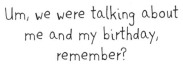

Um, we were talking about me and my birthday, remember?

Sorry, Sparrow!

It's OK.
Now remember when I made my wish?

Of course.
Did your wish come true yet?

Not yet.

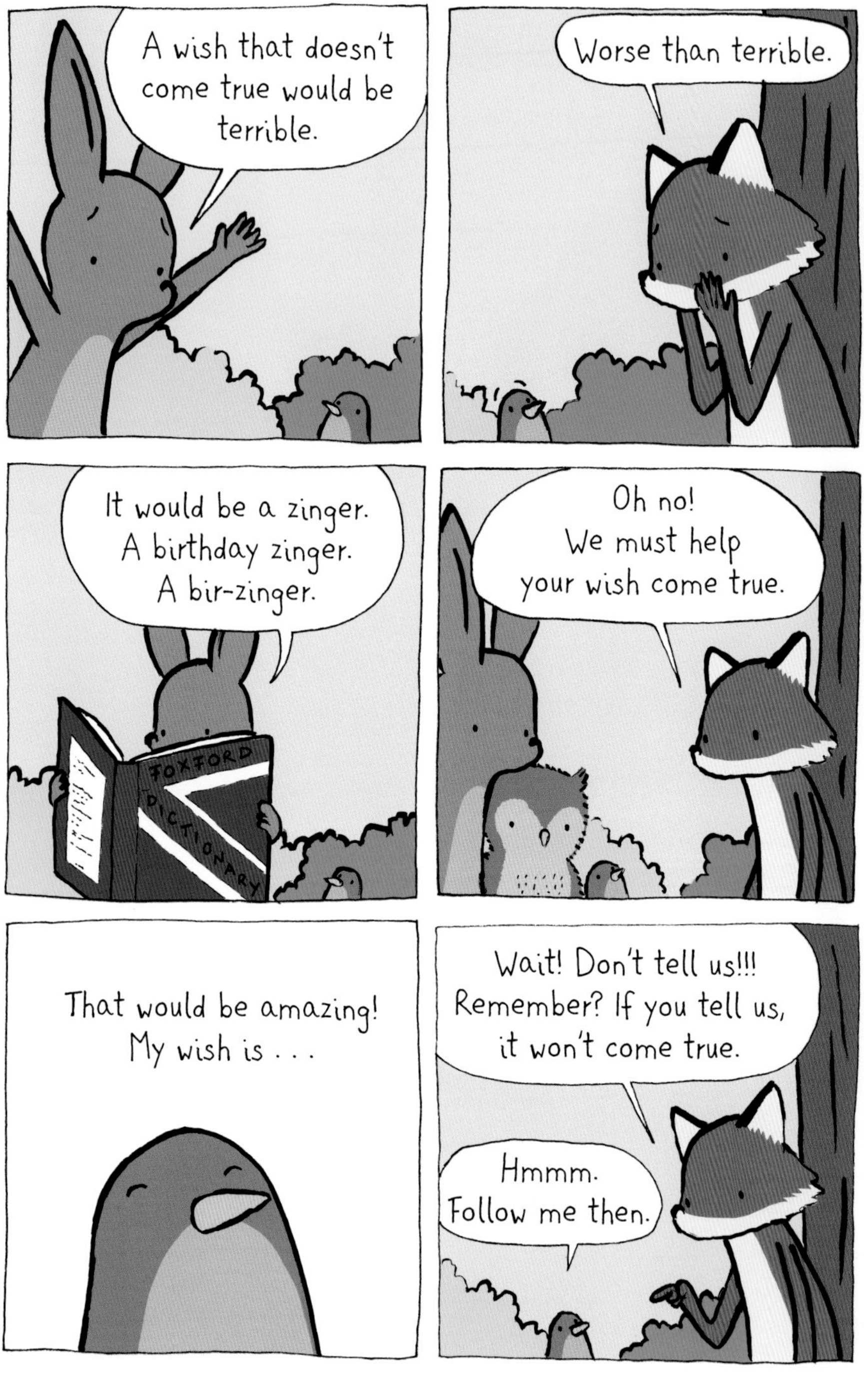
A wish that doesn't come true would be terrible.
Worse than terrible.
It would be a zinger. A birthday zinger. A bir-zinger.
FOXFORD DICTIONARY
Oh no! We must help your wish come true.
That would be amazing! My wish is . . .
Wait! Don't tell us!!! Remember? If you tell us, it won't come true.
Hmmm. Follow me then.

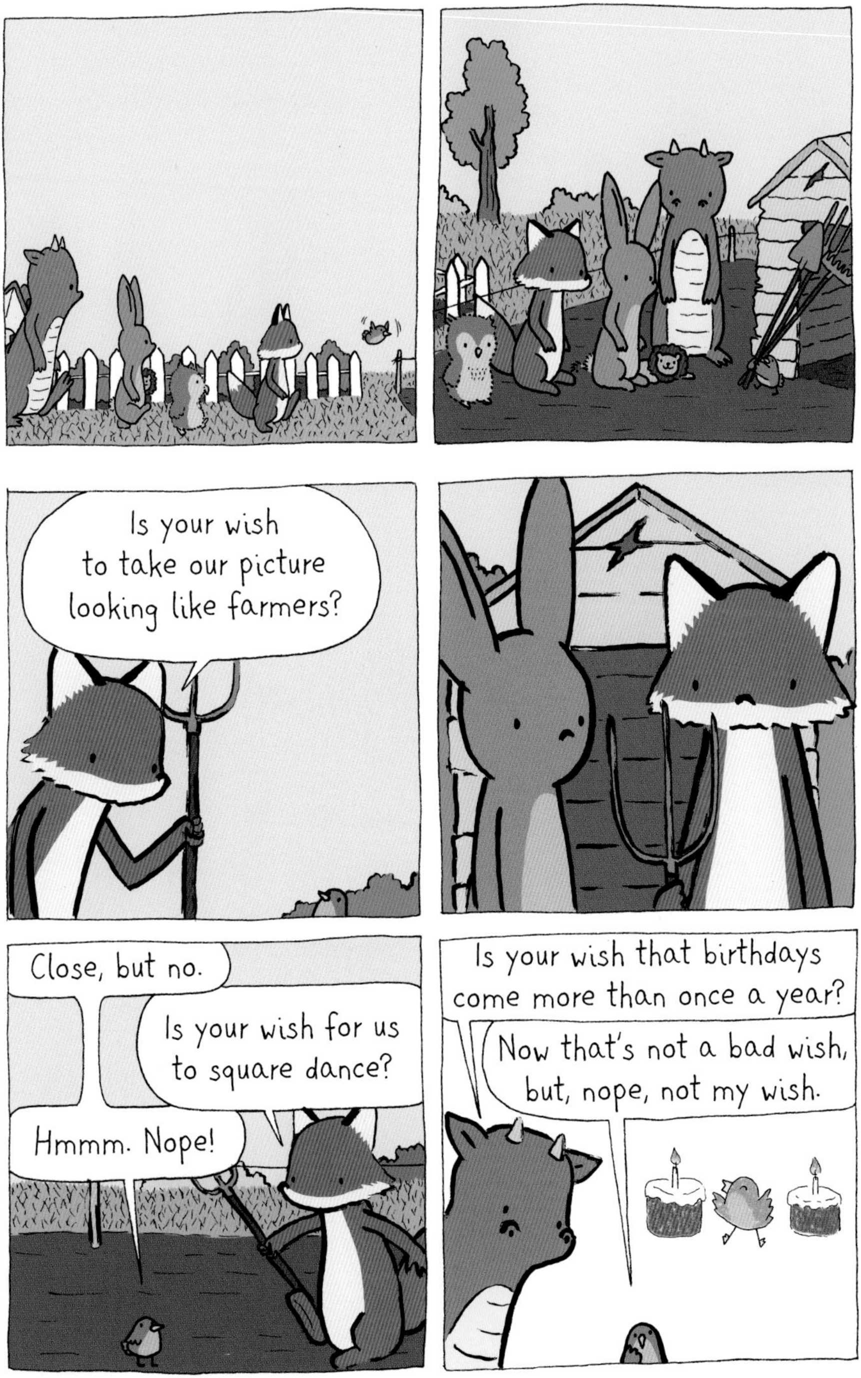

Is your wish to take our picture looking like farmers?
Close, but no.
Is your wish for us to square dance?
Hmmm. Nope!
Is your wish that birthdays come more than once a year?
Now that's not a bad wish, but, nope, not my wish.

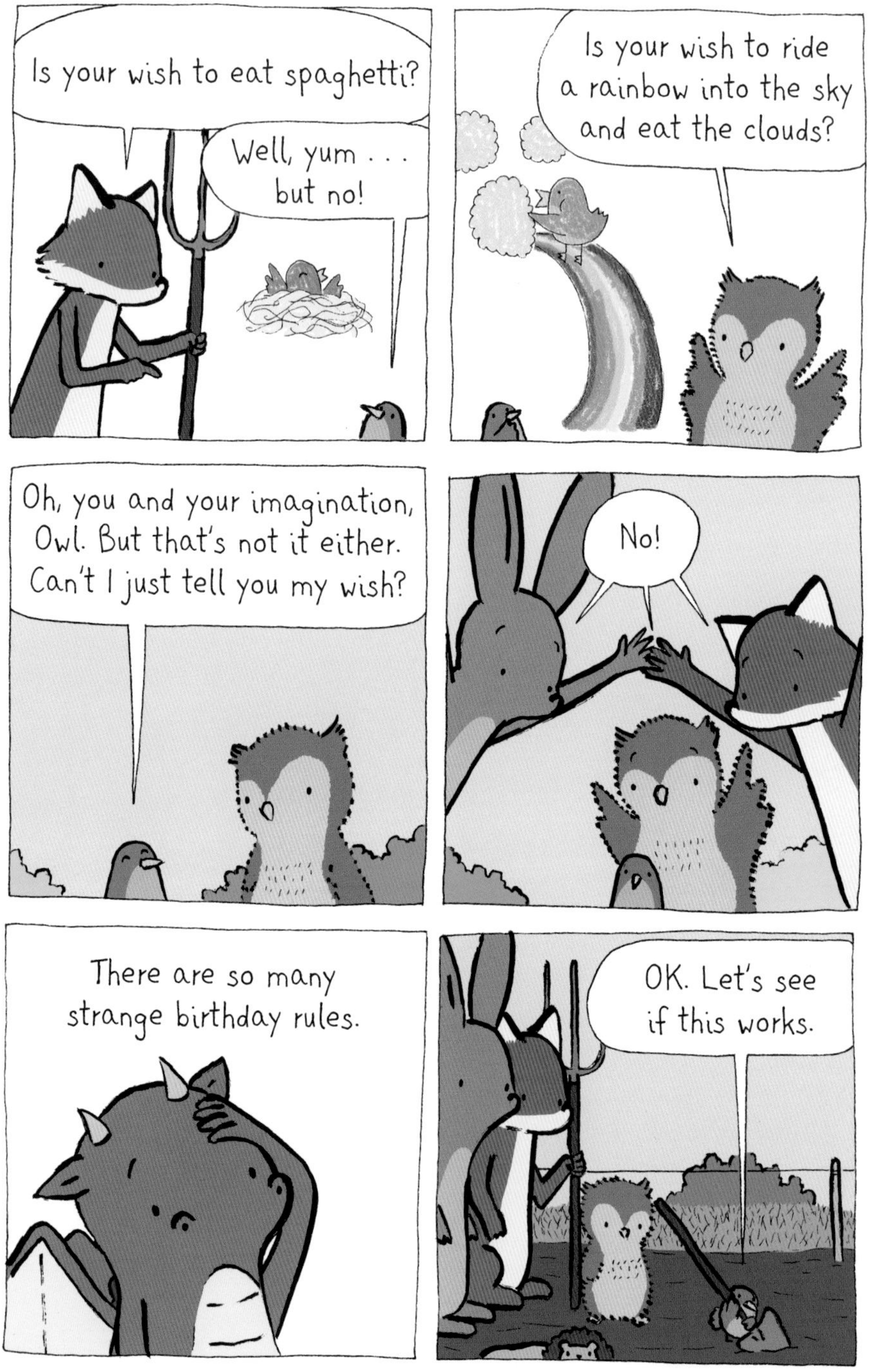
Is your wish to eat spaghetti?
Well, yum . . . but no!
Is your wish to ride a rainbow into the sky and eat the clouds?
Oh, you and your imagination, Owl. But that's not it either. Can't I just tell you my wish?
No!
There are so many strange birthday rules.
OK. Let's see if this works.

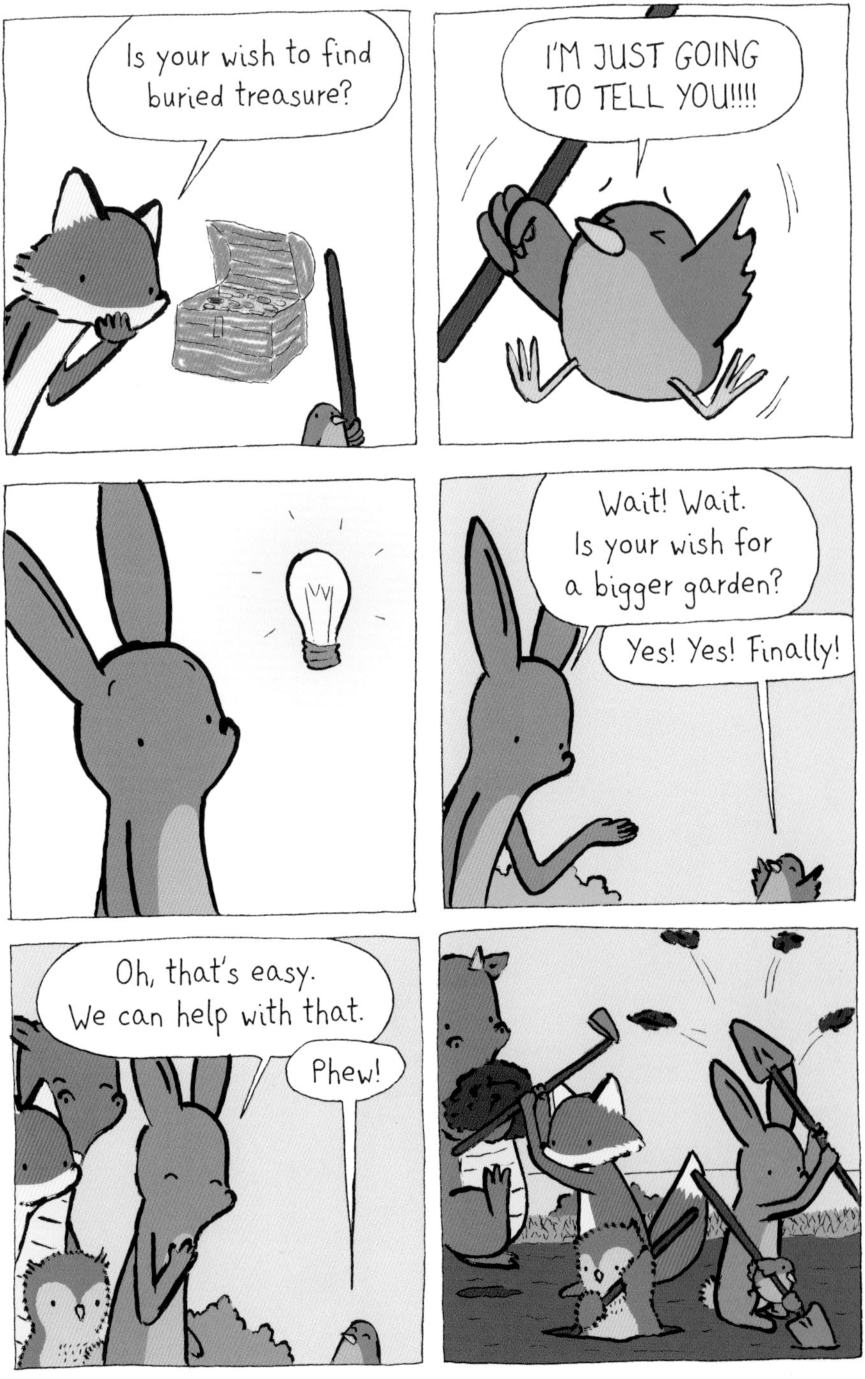
Is your wish to find buried treasure?
I'M JUST GOING TO TELL YOU!!!!
Wait! Wait. Is your wish for a bigger garden?
Yes! Yes! Finally!
Oh, that's easy. We can help with that.
Phew!

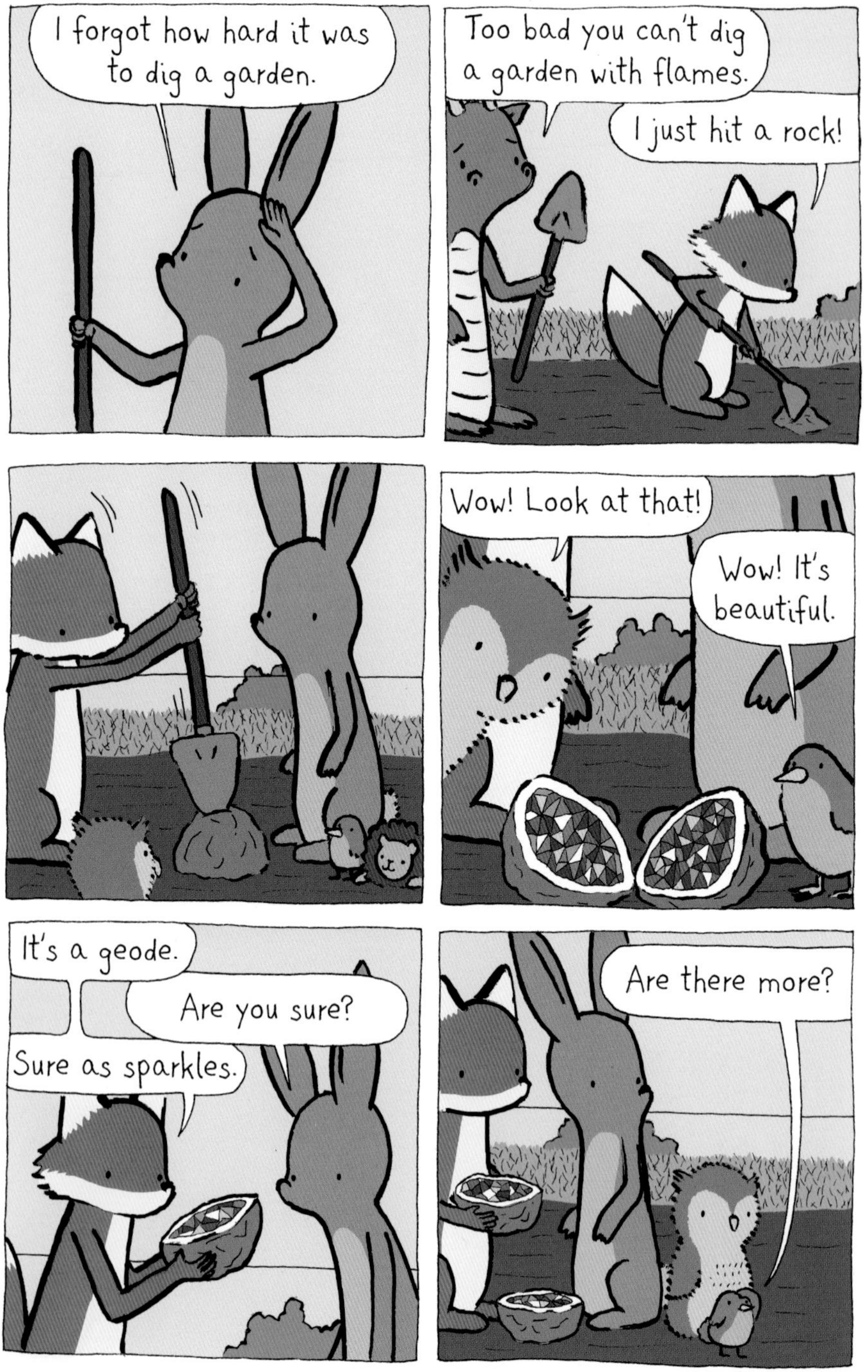
I forgot how hard it was to dig a garden.
Too bad you can't dig a garden with flames.
I just hit a rock!
Wow! Look at that!
Wow! It's beautiful.
It's a geode.
Are you sure?
Sure as sparkles.
Are there more?

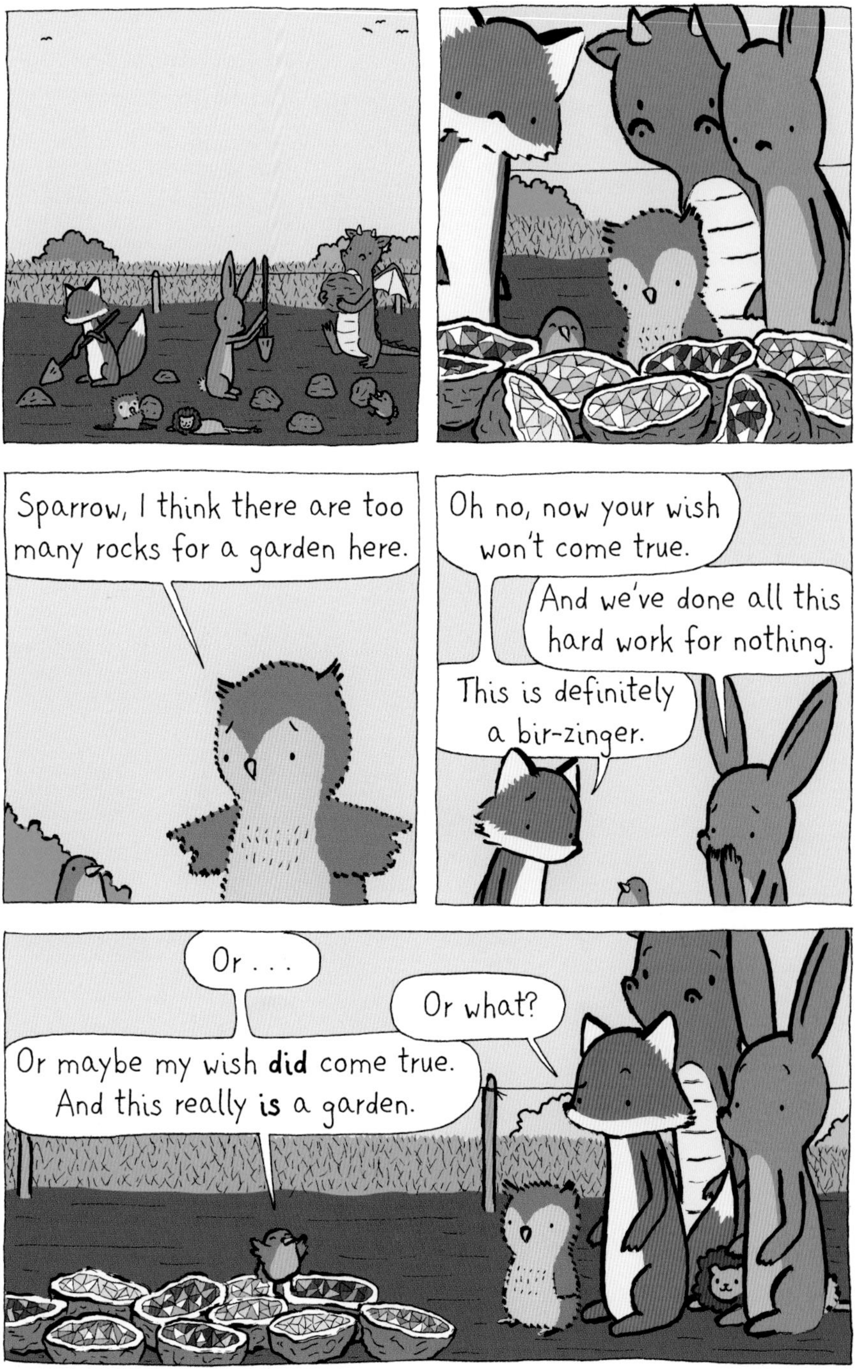
Sparrow, I think there are too many rocks for a garden here.
Oh no, now your wish won't come true.
And we've done all this hard work for nothing.
This is definitely a bir-zinger.
Or . . .
Or what?
Or maybe my wish **did** come true. And this really **is** a garden.

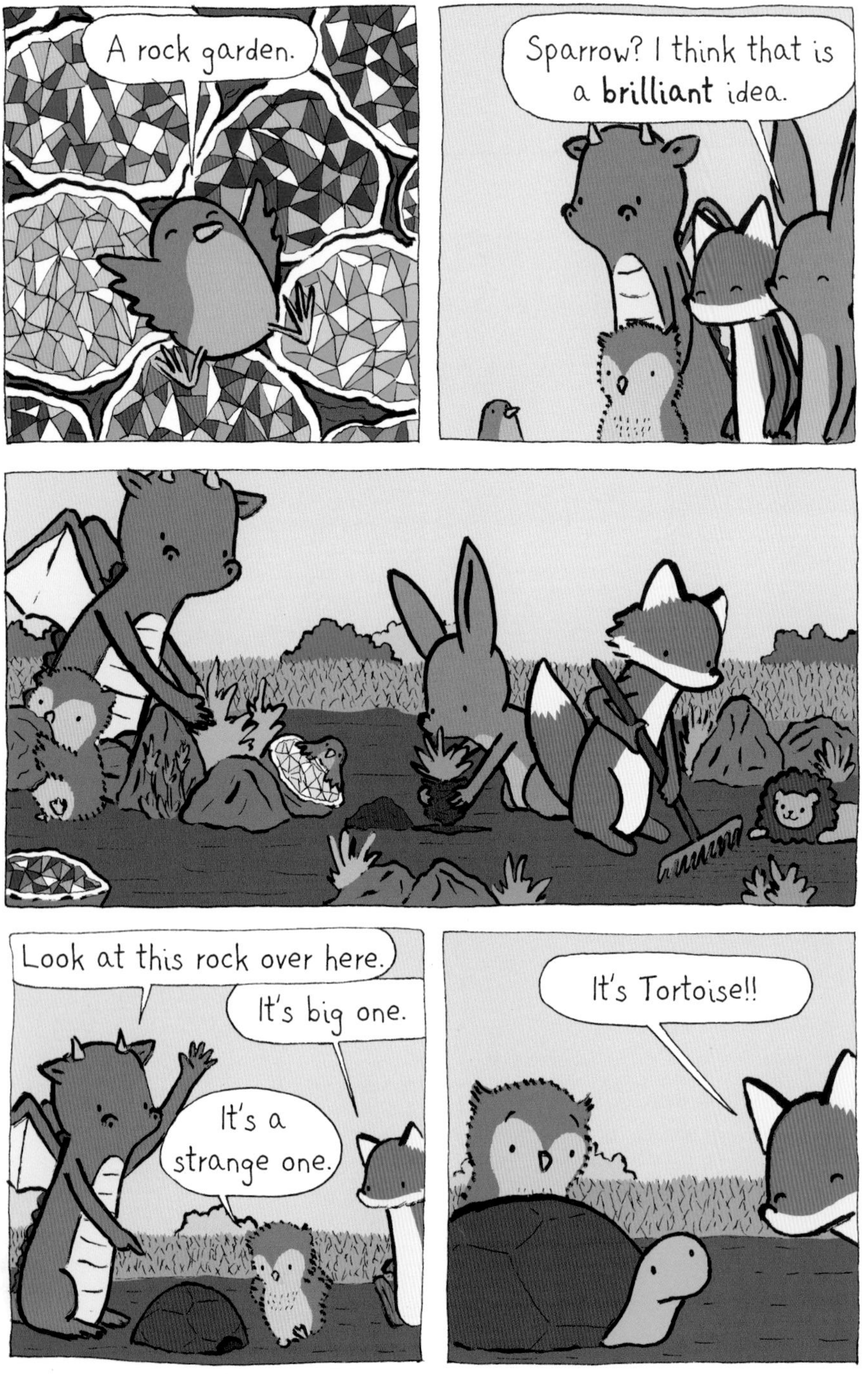
A rock garden.
Sparrow? I think that is a **brilliant** idea.
Look at this rock over here.
It's big one.
It's a strange one.
It's Tortoise!!

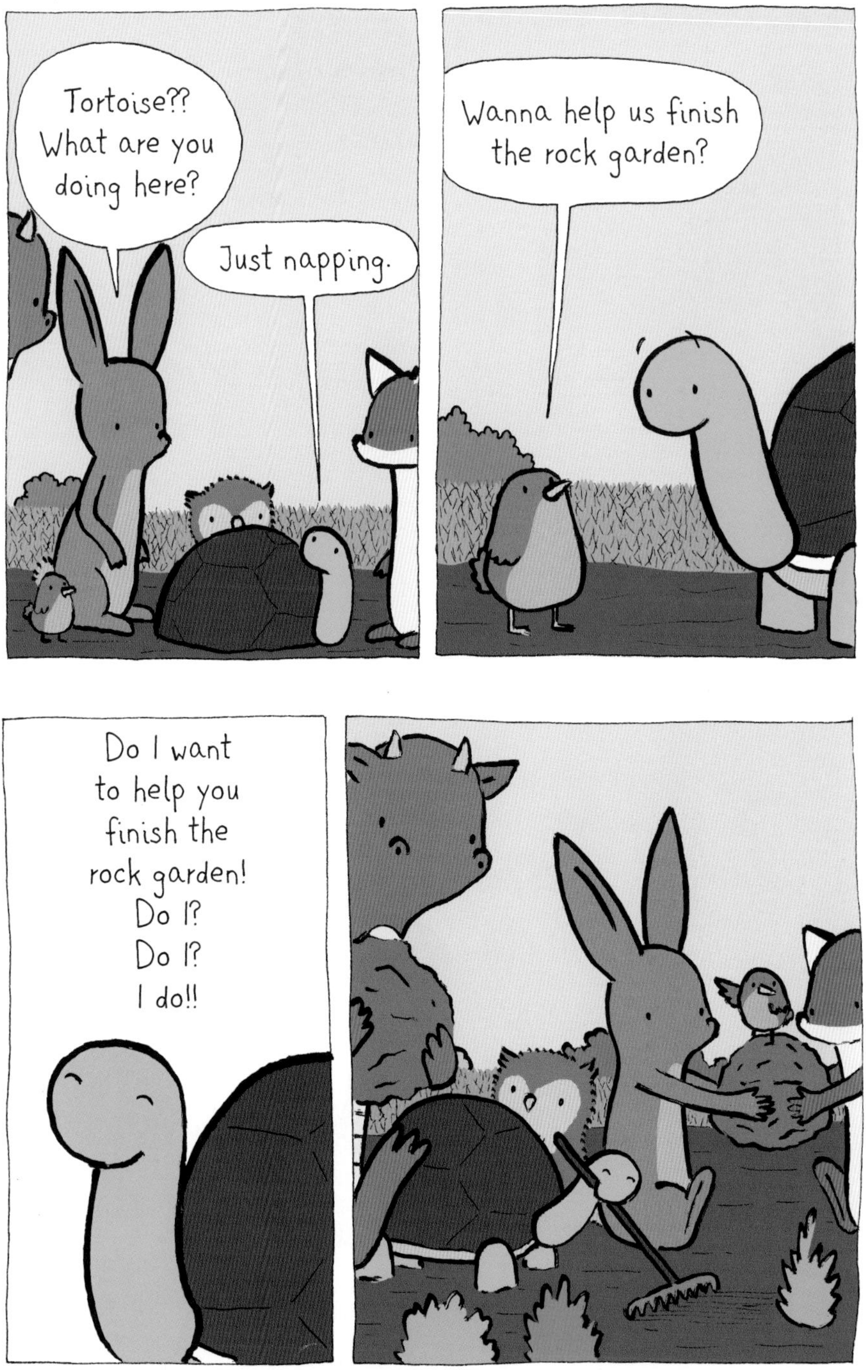
Tortoise?? What are you doing here?
Just napping.
Wanna help us finish the rock garden?
Do I want to help you finish the rock garden! Do I? Do I? I do!!

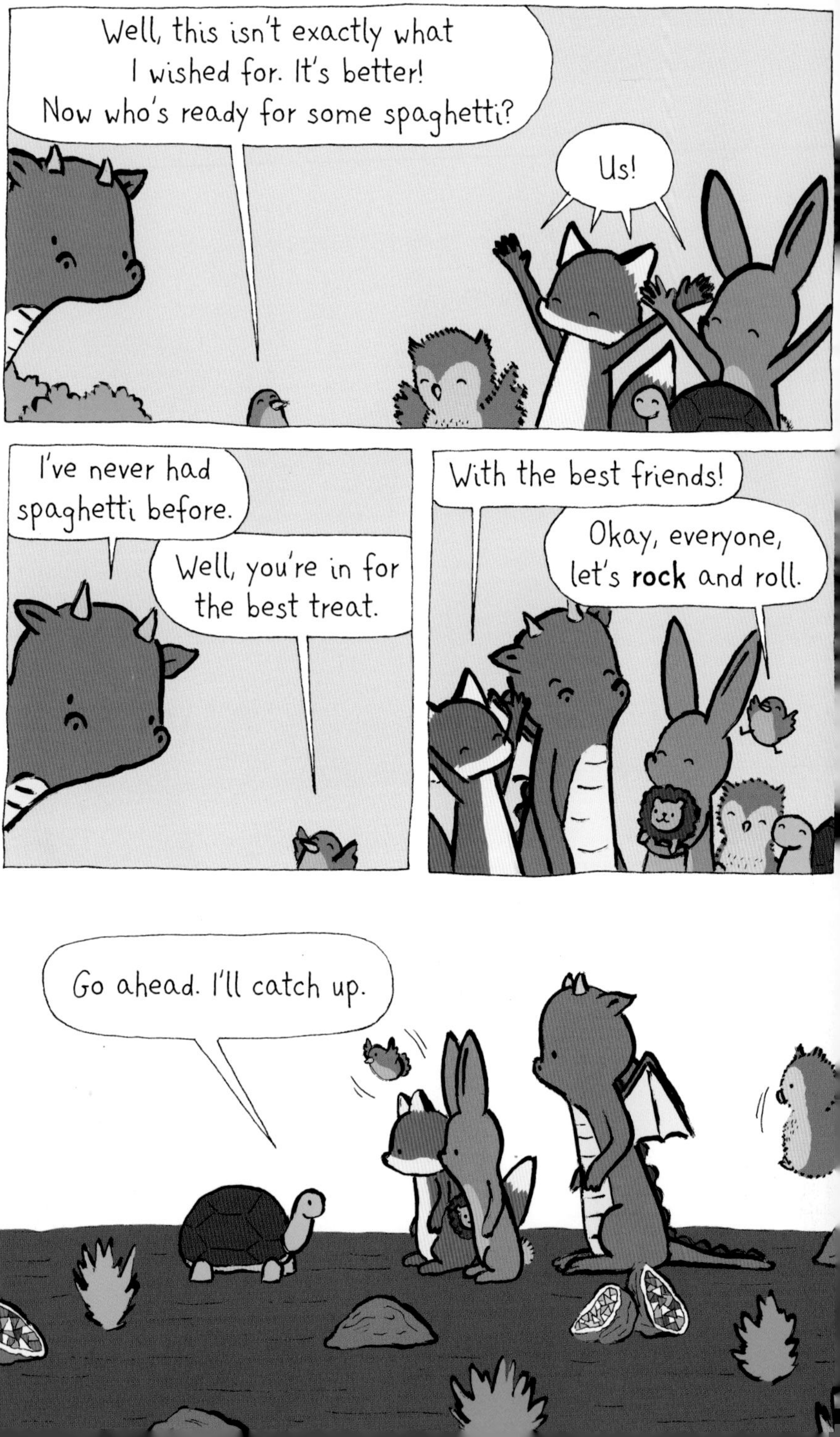
Well, this isn't exactly what I wished for. It's better! Now who's ready for some spaghetti?
Us!
I've never had spaghetti before.
Well, you're in for the best treat.
With the best friends!
Okay, everyone, let's **rock** and roll.
Go ahead. I'll catch up.

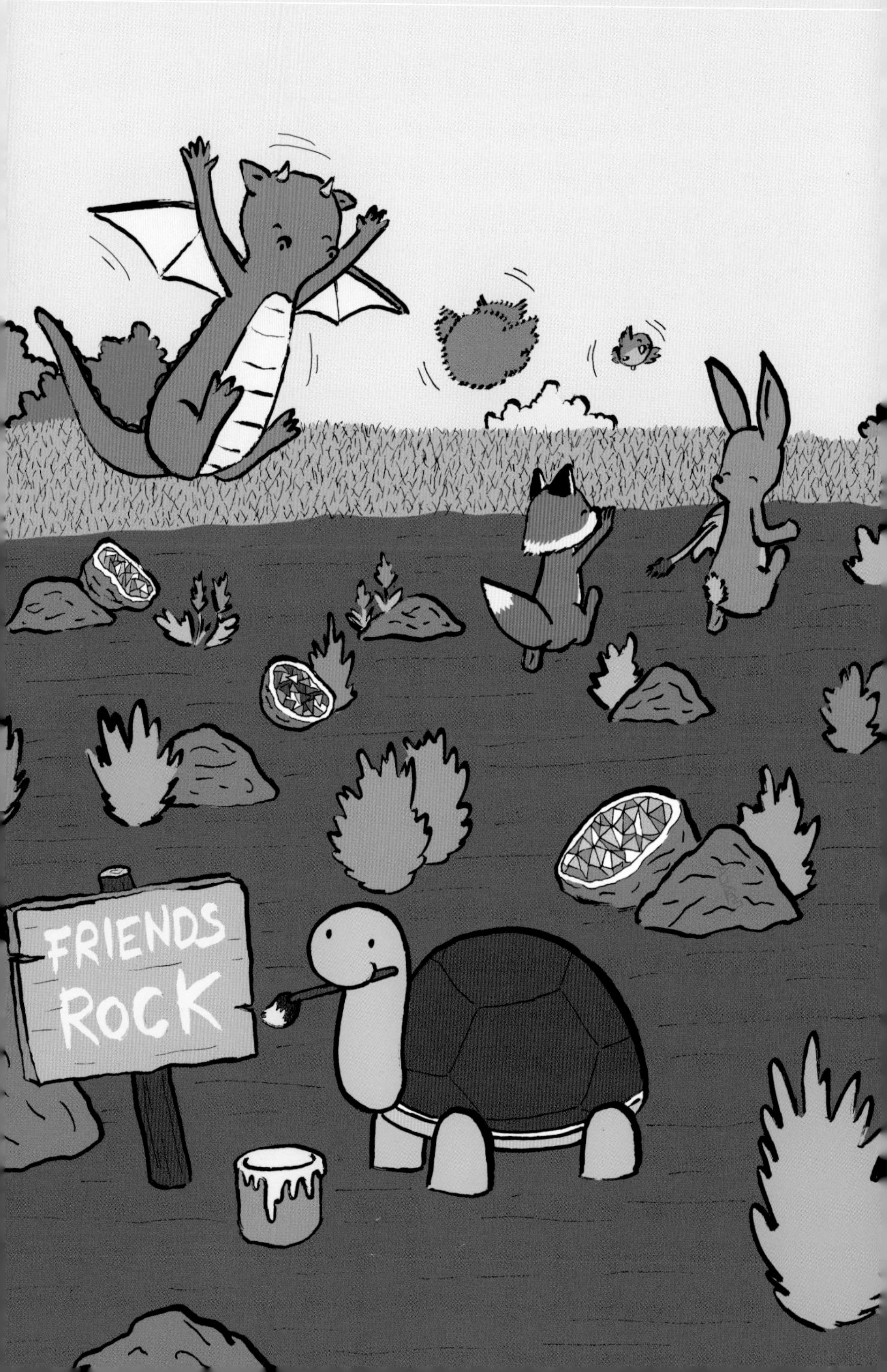
FRIENDS
ROCK

ABOUT THE AUTHOR

Beth Ferry celebrates the wonder of words and the magic of stories as the author of many books for young readers including the Fox & Rabbit series and myriad picture books illustrated by many talented artists. She lives by the beach in New Jersey where she celebrates summer and ice cream and friendship and reading and puppies and pizza and pumpkins. You can learn more at bethferry.com.

ABOUT THE ILLUSTRATOR

Gergely Dudás is a self-taught illustrator. He was born in July 1991. His artwork in the early 1990s was a lot more abstract than it is today. He is the creator of the Bear's Book of Hidden Things seek-and-find series.

Like Fox, Gergely likes fixing things. And like Sparrow, he loves celebrating, even the little things (for example, celebrating Sundays with crêpes). But unlike Rabbit, he doesn't know any dragons (yet).

He lives with his girlfriend and a dwarf rabbit called Fahéj.

Gergely's work is inspired by the magic of the natural world. You can see more from him at dudolf.com.

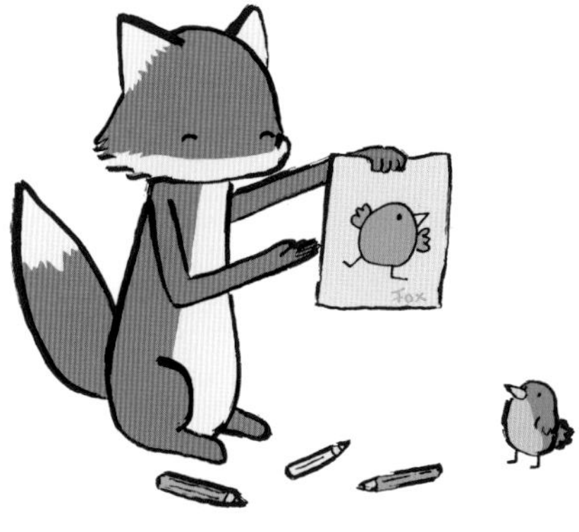
Fox

FOR JOSH, WHO GIVES US
SO MUCH TO CELEBRATE
—B.F.

FOR MY DEAR FRIEND VADI,
WHO APPRECIATES MY CHRISTMAS CARDS THE MOST
—G.D.

The art in this book was created with graphite and ink and colored digitally.

PUBLISHER'S NOTE: This is a work of fiction. Names, characters, places, and incidents are either the product of the author's imagination or used fictitiously, and any resemblance to actual persons, living or dead, business establishments, events, or locales is entirely coincidental.

Library of Congress Control Number 2020950724

ISBN 978-1-4197-5183-7

Text copyright © 2021 Beth Ferry
Illustrations copyright © 2021 Gergely Dudás
Book design by Heather Kelly

Printed and bound in China
10 9 8 7 6 5 4 3 2

Amulet Books are available at special discounts when purchased in quantity for premiums and promotions as well as fundraising or educational use. Special editions can also be created to specification. For details, contact specialsales@abramsbooks.com or the address below.

Amulet Books® is a registered trademark of Harry N. Abrams, Inc.

ABRAMS The Art of Books
195 Broadway, New York, NY 10007
abramsbooks.com